This book belongs to:

____

Keep your eyes peeled for the green Magical Elf Ticket inside your book to discover your *FREE Sleepy Elf guided meditation.*

The Lost Wish is an exciting story; you might want to read more than one chapter each night! You may be eager to read on and reluctant to go to sleep!

So why not listen to the Sleepy Elf-guided visualisation to help you relax?

You will join Remi the Sleepy Elf and set off on a magical sleep journey together.

You'll enjoy a gentle tour of the Sleepy Elf's Garden and meet some of Remi's friends as you drift off into a peaceful sleep.

The Lost Wish

Written By

Clare Anderson & Emily Jacobs

Illustrated By Emma Kurran

Book Bubble Press

The Lost Wish

Printed in the UK

Published by Book Bubble Press

First Published September 2022

ISBN: 978-1-912494-50-7

Book Bubble Press

books@bookbubblepress.com

www.bookbubblepress.com

For Siena

Thank you for your wonderful imagination. Your vision for Elf Eyes was the catalyst for this magical journey. You are, forever, the driving force in all that I do. Creating this story with you has been such a joy and your ideas, your energy and your zest for life are inspirational to me. I am so proud to be your mum.

I am a firm believer that people enter our lives for a reason. The Lost Wish journey has been no exception. This story has been brought to life by people who immediately understood our vision. Their talent has ensured that The Lost Wish is so much more than just an exciting story with a wealth of memorable characters.

Threads of wellness messages are woven into the tale to leave a lasting positive impression on young readers. Emily, Emma, Eloise, Sim, and Natalie, thank you!

Always in my thoughts and shining down on us, I must also thank my Rory star, a source of constant comfort and guidance from afar.

The Lost Wish

Meet the Characters

Eve (Siena)

Courageous, kind, and honest. Brimming with positivity and a sense of adventure.

Noelle (Gabi)

Excitable and full of wonder. She's a loyal friend with a heart of gold.

Meet the Characters

Buddy

Siena's loyal and loving pet dog. Boundless energy and always alert to danger *and* fun!

Perrie

A wise and beautiful Pixie with excellent flying skills. She is a Diminishing Dust and Growth Glitter expert.

Cookie & Pretzel

Cookie is an amazing baker! She runs the Sweet Treats Cafe... And dislikes rats.

Pretzel is the pastry chef at Sweet Treats Cafe and loves to sing and dance.

Meet the Characters

Eleuia (Ee-loo-ya)

The guardian of children's Star Wishes. Kind, clever and famous throughout Elfland.

Gizmo

Colour-changing dragon, Wish list hunter and airborne rescuer.

Coletta

An elf consumed by jealousy. Her own spell backfired and turned her into a Goblin.

Meet the Characters

Bow

Apprentice at the Leaf Factory and Eleuia's biggest fan. Caring, sensitive and eagle-eyed.

Lester

Elfland ticket collector and reluctant guide. Sometimes grumpy, especially when he's hungry... which is quite often.

Mr Arwin

Christmas stall holder, keeper of the Elfland map and wisest elf in the Wellness Woods.

Meet the Characters

Remi

Elfland's teleporting, telepathic Sleep Elf- the keeper of the grand sleep secret. The Sleep Elf's mesmerising voice helps children everywhere relax, rest, and enjoy the best sleep ever!

Genie

Brilliant Elfland engineer and inventor. The ONLY elf authorised to drive Santa's sleigh.

Beanie

Genie's energetic pet, rat-botherer and Christmas gift delivery expert.

Meet the Characters

Bing and Tinsel

Cheeky twins. They look after the sorting office portal where children's wishes arrive. Bing is fluent in every language of the world and Tinsel is very intuitive. She can sense the emotions of others.

Miss Jolly

Boss of Elfland Adventures and yoga expert. She adores her fellow elves and always has a kind and caring word for everyone she meets.

Meet the Characters

Santa

World famous Christmas icon and Elfland celebrity.

He needs no introduction!

Prologue

She folded her arms on the windowsill, rested her chin, and pressed the tip of her nose against the cold windowpane. Plump snowflakes had begun twirling out of the grey afternoon sky and she watched them drift and settle on the garden path. Siena tried to count the dark wet splodges left behind as they melted, but there were too many and even she couldn't count *that* fast! Besides, more and more flakes were surviving the landing and the cold stones were soon hiding beneath a thin white blanket.

It was another thrilling sign that Santa would soon be on his way.

The last few days of school had been filled with end-of-term shows, carol concerts, festive crafts, and lots of happy chatter. Christmas magic filled the air and Siena was so excited, that she'd found it difficult to get to sleep this week. When sleep had finally arrived, however, she had enjoyed vivid and wonderful dreams. Last night, colourful elves welcomed her to a beautiful forest. She had huddled together with them in cosy friendship and toasted marshmallows around a glowing fire. In the night sky above, a single star shone warm and bright, and Siena needed to shield her eyes to look up at it. As she did so, she'd been rudely awoken by the rays of winter sunshine beaming through a gap in her bedroom curtains.

Now, gazing at the falling snow, Siena wondered what Santa's elves might be up to. They must be very busy wrapping all the presents. How *did* they make all those gifts *and* deliver them in time? And did they really work hard every day, all year round, to make children's wishes come true? Surely not, thought Siena. All work and no play wasn't good for anyone. There must be a place and a time for them to relax and have fun.

Suddenly, Siena heard her mother's voice from downstairs. It was time to go. She, and her best friend Gabi, had been talking about this trip to the Christmas market all week. Afterwards, they were having a sleepover and the secret midnight feast was already stored safely in her bedside drawer.

Siena snatched up her coat and picked her way across a bedroom floor that was littered with books of all shapes and sizes.

"Coming Mum!" she called.

This was going to be so much fun!

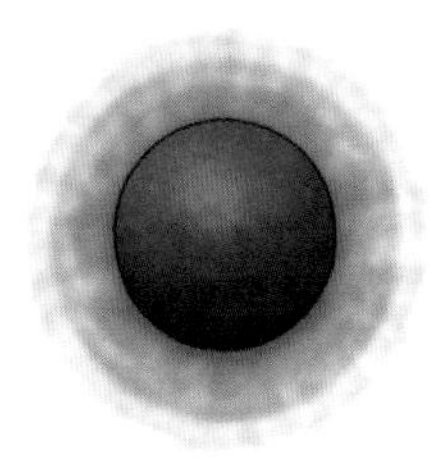

Chapter 1

The magical market stall

'That's strange,' said Arthur, 'you don't normally see butterflies in winter.'

Albie paused while he attempted to catch a snowflake on his tongue. 'Well, it looked like a bumble bee to me,' he said.

The flicker of fast-moving light caught ten-year-old Siena's eye. She had no idea what it was, but she knew it was *not* a butterfly *or* a bumblebee. It danced away and disappeared amongst the market stalls, where the grown-ups were browsing for Christmas gifts.

'You're both wrong,' said Gabi, waving away their ideas, 'it was *definitely* a dragonfly.' She came to a sudden stop. 'Never mind that though. Look!' She pointed excitedly at the enormous, decorated fir tree in the middle of the square. A large gathering of people, wrapped up in scarves and hats, had encircled the tree, eagerly awaiting the big Christmas light switch on.

The countdown had already begun.

'...six, five, four, three, two, one...' The crowd joined in the chant. The centre of the normally quiet country town was alive with magic.

The mayor threw the oversized switch and instantly, the town square was illuminated with a thousand twinkling lights. People in the crowd gasped and clapped as carol-singers on the makeshift stage launched into a rendition of 'Santa Claus is Coming to Town'. Albie was thrilled about this, until his older brother, Arthur, reminded him that there were a few more sleeps before the big day.

On arrival at the Christmas market, the children had been given five pounds each to spend at the stalls. Their parents had given strict instructions to stay together and not to go out of sight. The children looked around. All the stalls had solid wooden frames with festive decorations and strings of pretty fairy lights. There were raffles, tombola's, Christmas baubles, cakes, and candles – and a farmer had brought his reindeer for children to feed and pet. You could even have your photo taken with them. Arthur was fascinated and he handed over his money immediately.

Meanwhile, Gabi followed her nose and made a beeline for the cake stand. Aunt Betty's Bakery had a stall on the pavement, and they were selling the most delicious-looking Christmas muffins. Gabi bought four for five pounds and she let Siena and Albie choose one each from the paper bag. They were still warm, and the children munched happily.

'Sooo good.' Gabi smiled, unable to resist eating the last one. She wiped the sugary frosting from her mouth. A few metres away, Arthur was too busy hugging Rudolph to realise he'd missed out on a sweet treat.

Siena knew where *she* was going first – the arts and crafts tent. Every year, art teacher Miss Clarke ran a competition. This year, it was all about creating your own spirit elf. The pictures would be displayed in the school reception area, and the winner announced on the last day of term. The prize was a mystery hamper full of goodies.

'Hello, you lovely lot.' Miss Clarke grinned as they approached. She had blonde, shoulder-length hair, and a welcoming smile and all the children adored her. To ward off the cold, she was wearing a bright orange jacket and a matching bobble hat. The seats around the table were filling up fast. Eager children were waiting for their instructions.

Pens, glue sticks, glitter pots and all sorts of arts and crafts materials were spread before them, ready for them to create their masterpieces.

Miss Clarke began. 'If you were an elf, what elf name would you choose? Would you have a superpower? What would your outfit be like and what would your special act of kindness be? Use all your wonderful imagination because there is no right or wrong answer. Just have fun! Once you've finished your artwork, pop your name on the back and pass it to me.' Dozens of small hands scrabbled for the materials they would need.

Siena and Gabi selected green and red pens from the jar in front of them. Siena loved gymnastics and cheerleading, they were her favourite activities, and she wondered if maybe she'd give her elf super strength so she could jump and flip higher and faster.

'Noelle,' said Gabi. 'I love the name Noelle, and my superpower will be the ability to fly off to magical lands.' She giggled. She loved spending time with friends and was always happy on an adventure.

The girls got to work drawing their elves.

'I think my elf name would be Eve,' said Siena, writing *Eve* on the elf hat she had designed, 'and I would have a star-shaped wand to grant wishes.' She carefully drew the outline of the wand.

Just as the girls were finishing up, Siena felt a sudden, sharp tug on her sleeve. It was an excited Arthur with Albie just behind. 'Come on,' he said breathlessly. 'Quick!' Arthur tugged again on Siena's red coat, knocking over the pen jar in his haste. 'Sorry!' he blurted, hurriedly picking it up and shoving the pens back into the container.

'Thanks, Miss Clarke!' chorused the girls as they passed their pictures over and climbed off the wooden stools. Arthur was already off and running, darting in and out of the crowds. The others had to move fast to keep up.

'Wait! Where are we going?' called Siena. They were running in the direction of her parents, who were shopping at the decorations stall. 'Arthur is showing us something!' Siena called as they charged past.

'Slow down, children! And you have fifteen minutes!' Siena's mum shouted after them, laughing at their urgency.

Arthur wasn't listening. The children's snow boots clumped noisily on the pavement as they charged after him. Several sharp turns later, on the edge of the market, Arthur came to an abrupt, skidding stop. Albie, Siena, and Gabi bumped into him and all four tumbled to the floor like dominoes.

'Arthur!' shouted Gabi, wiping muddy snow from her new blue coat. Ignoring their breathless grumbles, Arthur pointed. 'Look!

They found themselves in a lane containing just one stall, and it was the most fabulous stall the children had seen so far.

The flickering flames of the candles hanging inside the lanterns gave off a warm glow and lit up a beautiful wooden table that was scattered with curious artefacts.

Seated behind the magnificent table was a small, white-haired man wearing a sumptuous blue velvet cloak. He had silver-rimmed spectacles sitting on the end of his nose and, darting and dancing around his head, was the strange light the children had spotted and wondered about when they first arrived. Siena, Gabi, Arthur, and Albie had lived on the same street and had known each other since they were very little. They had never seen anything like this, and curiosity was churning inside them.

The little man in the blue cloak raised one wizened hand. The ball of light darted towards it and suddenly it was gone.

'Magic!' the children gasped.

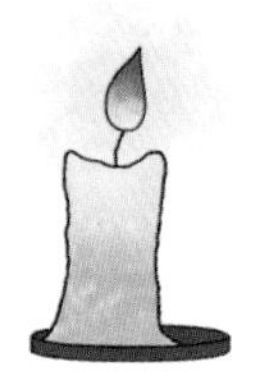

Chapter 2

Smells like Christmas

The children gaped at the curious little man. Gabi guessed that, if he stood up, he would only be the same height as her. His face was weathered and wrinkly and he had a luxuriant, snow-white beard that reached all the way to his waist. As Siena moved closer, she noticed his ice-blue eyes that sparkled in the light from the many lanterns arranged around him. He greeted the children with a broad smile and beckoned them closer.

'It smells like Christmas,' whispered Gabi as she breathed in the scent curling from thin sticks that were smouldering in a small bowl on the table. The light from the lanterns flickered and danced in the cold breeze.

'And what does Christmas smell like?' asked the man, removing his blue velvet hood to reveal a shock of white hair.

'Like cinnamon and pine trees,' Gabi replied, wafting the fragrance towards her nose.

'I think it smells like hot chocolate.' Albie grinned,

thinking of the steaming mug of hot chocolate with whipped cream and marshmallows that he'd be having on Christmas Eve.

Arthur said nothing. He was busy looking over the man's shoulder, searching the back of the market stall for the curious light that seemed to have just disappeared. He had watched a TV show all about illusions, and how they were done, so he knew it *must* be hidden somewhere.

Siena smiled at the man and picked up a plain wooden spoon from the table. It looked out of place amongst the other fascinating things. She held it in her gloved hands, inspecting it carefully. *Why would anyone buy a plain old wooden spoon?*

As if reading her mind, the old man said, 'Ah, a simple wooden spoon. It could be a sword to protect you against trolls and goblins, or perhaps a wand to grant wishes. It really can be anything you believe it to be.'

Siena smiled politely but she wasn't convinced and carefully placed the wooden spoon back on the table. Her attention was drawn to an intriguing box. Printed on the side were the words, 'Elf Eyes'. Gabi and Albie were momentarily distracted by snowballs that Arthur had just launched towards the patch of grass behind the stalls. Several children they recognised from school were engaged in a snowball fight in the light thrown by the Christmas market.

Siena glanced across at her friends as they raced

onto the snowball battlefield, and then she returned her attention to the man and his table of treasures. She still had her five pounds to spend. She picked up the inviting red and green box, which she now noticed was also decorated with elf characters that skipped and danced around the sides.

'A most excellent choice, young lady,' said the man, gleefully. 'The magical Elf Eyes. Buy them, and I'll throw in the wooden spoon and even a hat for free!' He pointed to a ragged woolly hat that was hanging on the wall of the market stall. It looked like it had seen better days.

Siena eyed the wooden spoon and the green hat. She wasn't sure she needed those items, but the funny man seemed kind and he was most insistent. 'Thank you,' she said, handing over the money. He rummaged in a wooden box for the right change and tipped a few coins into Siena's outstretched hand. Siena heard familiar voices and turned around.

'Home time!' Their parents were calling and waving to them. Had it been fifteen minutes already? Siena tucked her purchases under one arm and waved back, acknowledging that she had heard. Turning towards the snowball fight, she called to her friends.

'Come on, you guys. It's time to go. Sleepover time, Gabi!'

Arthur, Albie, and Gabi threw their last snowballs and, laughing and stumbling, raced towards Siena.

Siena turned back to the market stall, but the mysterious little man was gone, and so were all his belongings. All that remained was the beautiful, but now empty, wooden table gleaming in the light of the lanterns. She leaned over the counter and peered underneath, but the little man was nowhere to be seen. Very peculiar. On the way home, Siena wondered if it had been real, unexplainable magic. But Arthur confidently insisted it was all an illusion and that he would learn the tricks and show them how it was done.

Chapter 3

The deep sleep

At the garden gate, Siena and Gabi waved goodbye to Arthur and Albie and hurried into the house, tearing off scarves, hats, and gloves as they went. Siena's dog, Buddy, barked and bounced excitedly at their return and they both ruffled his ears and made a fuss of him. In the kitchen, Siena's dad made them hot drinks and they warmed their hands on steaming mugs of delicious hot chocolate before heading upstairs to get ready for bed. Buddy, as ever, followed their every move. He finally flopped down on a blanket in the corner of the bedroom as the girls clambered into the sleepover den they'd constructed from beanbags and pillows.

'I don't think I'll be able to sleep,' Siena whispered.

'Neither will I,' agreed Gabi.

Siena's room was already filled with Christmas spirit and a long string of fairy lights twinkled over and around the bookcase where a thousand stories tumbled from the shelves. Siena flicked on her bedside lamp and stars turned gently across the ceiling. Gabi stumbled from the mountain of pillows and fetched the sleepover midnight feast from a bedside drawer. Soon, the sweet smell of popcorn filled the room. It set Buddy's nose twitching and he padded across the rug in search of a snack. The two girls wriggled into sleeping bags.

As they munched popcorn and homemade cookies under the stars, Siena reached for the box she had bought from the mysterious little man at the Christmas market. She found instructions on the side and began to read aloud.

'Elf Eyes – transport you from the fun festivities to heavenly relaxation... a warm hug for tired eyes. Elf Eyes are magical eye masks that only heat up when you open the packet. Tap the mask packet three times and say, "Elf Eyes come alive, sparkle and shine, warm up and be mine".'

Siena opened the box carefully.

'There's a green ticket here,' she said, passing it to Gabi.

Gabi turned it over in her hands and sat up. 'Not just any ticket,' she said. 'A *winning* ticket! How exciting! I wonder what you win?'

Siena continued reading and gasped. 'It says here, "You've won a trip to Elfland"!'

Outside, the weather had taken a turn for the worse and a flurry of sleet and snow now pattered sharply at the rattling window. They snuggled down and reached for another delicious cookie. Then a sudden flicker of light that flashed across the room froze their hands in mid-air. It happened so quickly that it could easily have been missed but it stopped the two girls in their tracks, and they stared at each other. Buddy gave a bark and sprang up to investigate. He paced the room and nosed into the corner where the light seemed to have gone.

Gabi wriggled quickly down into her sleeping bag and pulled it sharply over her head.

'What was that?' she whispered.

Siena peered at the night light that was still turning gently beside them, sending pinpricks of starlight across the walls and ceiling.

'Oh nothing,' she said. 'Probably just this old thing finally packing up. I think it's a bit broken. It sometimes sends big shooting stars across the room!' She called to Buddy. He completed his investigations and lay down across the girls' feet. His presence was comforting.

'You can come out now, Gabi.' Siena giggled.

Gabi emerged slowly and stared wide-eyed around the room. She wasn't sure what had just happened, and she wasn't quite convinced by her friend's explanation either.

'Let's try these Elf Eyes,' said Siena, reaching for the box once more. 'It says they're relaxing.'

She raised the wooden spoon that the mysterious man had included in the market stall deal and followed the instructions, tapping the Elf Eyes sachet three times, and chanting, 'Elf Eyes come alive, sparkle and shine, warm up and be mine.'

She said the magic words again before carefully unwrapping the masks. Together, the children put them on. The masks felt soft and comforting and. they had little strings that tucked behind the ears to keep them securely in place. Siena and Gabi lay back, rested their heads on their pillows and enjoyed the gentle warmth that began to flow through the eye masks. It was just like a cosy hug, and they felt their bodies relax. *Magic.*

Once more, they chanted together, 'Elf Eyes come alive, sparkle and shine, warm up and be mine.' This time, their words came as drowsy whispers. They felt their bodies growing heavy and they had soon fallen into a deep and comfortable sleep.

Magical Elf Ticket

ElfLand uk

ELF GREETINGS TO THE FINDER OF THIS MAGICAL TICKET

CONGRATULATIONS!

THIS TICKET GIVES YOU ACCESS TO A SLEEPY ELF GUIDED MEDITATION TRACK

Just ask permission from a parent or guardian and scan the QR code below.

Chapter 4

A flutter of tiny wings

They were startled awake not by the alarm, or by Siena's mother calling to them up the stairs, but by the sound of scampering tiny feet and the annoying buzz of a large insect.

No longer tucked up tight in their sleeping bags,

Siena and Gabi found themselves on a woodland path in the warm winter sunshine. They were still in their pyjamas with Buddy standing nearby, sniffing the air. They gaped at each other. Were they dreaming? But how could they both be in the same dream at the same time? And the pebbly path beneath their feet certainly felt very real.

The sound of scampering footsteps came again. Buddy gave a low growl and the girls looked around for the source of the noise. A sudden flicker of light shot up from the path to eye level and there, hovering in the air before them, buzzing loudly, was the most remarkable sight.

'A fairy!' squealed Gabi, delighted. Buddy barked and leapt, snapping his jaws at the curious tiny creature. Siena reached for his collar.

'Oh, my goodness, no! I'm a pixie, not a tooth-collecting fairy!' she said with a giggle. 'You may call me Perrie.'

The girls stared in wonder. The pixie was no taller than a teaspoon but breathtakingly beautiful and her silver wings seemed to flutter effortlessly behind her. Long blonde hair was tucked behind dainty pointed ears and her hairband, adorned with ruby jewels, looked like a tiny crown. She looked from Siena to Gabi with mischievous eyes and played to her captivated audience. She pirouetted gracefully in the air, showing off the flowing red dress that looked fit for a princess.

'I can't believe that young boy thought I was a bumblebee,' she said with a giggle. 'I mean bumblebees *are* very clever of course, but I look nothing like one, as you can see.'

Siena and Gabi were dumbstruck. This had to be a dream, surely. And yet in that moment they realised this pixie was the strange light they had seen dance and dart at the Christmas market. It already seemed a long time ago. Another time and place.

'Are you ready to enter Elfland?' Perrie asked, tipping her head to one side and gesturing along the path. They had been so transfixed by the pixie, they hadn't had the chance to take in their surroundings or to notice what looked like a grand entrance just a short distance away.

Twisted tree branches on either side of the path formed an enticing archway decorated with pretty lights. From the arch, there hung a large wooden sign and on it, in beautiful flowing red script, was written one word...

Elfland

Perrie turned and fluttered away towards it. The girls glanced at each other, wide-eyed with wonder and gingerly followed their new pixie friend. Their bare feet were not suited to the pebbly path. Buddy stayed close to Siena, obedient and protective. They felt very small and insignificant as they approached the towering entrance. Above them, the Elfland sign creaked gently in the breeze.

On the other side, as far as the eye could see, there was forest. A light dusting of snow blanketed the ground. All was quiet and though the trees were densely packed, the woodland floor was illuminated by warm sunbeams breaching the leaves and branches above. Gabi was ready for an adventure, and she gripped Siena's arm excitedly. Perrie turned to the girls with a stern look. 'In order to enter Elfland, you must say some magic words. Repeat them after me.'

I close my eyes and count to three,
I dream big and I believe,
In myself, in magic, and kindness too,
Elfland adventures I'm ready for you!

Siena and Gabi held hands tightly and closed their eyes. They stepped forward nervously, repeating the magic words as they entered Elfland. A cool wind swirled around them and ruffled their hair. Eyes tightly closed, they felt light as feathers, floating just above the snowy path. Then, with the final words of the rhyme, they found their feet firmly back on the ground. Slowly, they opened their eyes.

Chapter 5

The dragon in the shadows

'We're elves!' cried Siena and Gabi, joyfully admiring their new outfits.

Their pyjamas had been replaced with the most wonderful green dresses. The red collars were trimmed with gold and the same glittering thread had been used on the hems. Wide black belts with golden buckles were wrapped around their middles and bejewelled slippers now protected their feet from the stony path. Siena noticed that, tucked into her belt was a simple wooden spoon. The girls' brown hair was now in perfect plaits; Siena's hung down her back, whilst Gabi's sat on her shoulders.

'Elf-tastic! Your name's Noelle,' cried Siena, pointing at the word embroidered on Gabi's hat.

'And you're not Siena anymore. You're Eve!' said Gabi, bursting with excitement.

'Elf names only in Elfland please,' said Perrie as she fluttered around, inspecting the two girls. 'And keep your elf hat on at *all* times. A good elf never takes off their hat.' The girls chuckled at Buddy who was modelling an elf hat of his own. It had a small brass bell, and he was frantically swinging his head to try and work out where the jingle was coming from.

'Why?' asked Noelle, grateful her hat was comfy if she couldn't take it off.

'An elf hat is like a badge of honour. Not all elves have hats. They only receive one on entering Elfland,' Perrie explained. The girls shrugged and smiled. Their hats were lovely and warm, so they were happy to keep them on, especially with a snowy chill in the air.

There was a cough. 'Ahem!' said a gruff voice. 'Are you coming in or not?'

Just to one side of the path, there was yet another bizarre sight. Leaning against a sort of golden letter box, was a rat. But this was no ordinary rodent. He was wearing a tight red waistcoat that was straining to stay buttoned over a very round tummy. His matching hat was at a jaunty angle and its tiny brass bell jingled as he thrust out a paw.

'Tickets?' he said.

'Oh. This is Lester,' sighed Perrie. 'He's our rather *impatient* Elfland gatekeeper I'm afraid.' She pointedly raised her eyebrows at the plump little creature. 'Children visit Elfland quite often, but Lester has yet to learn his manners! Please hand over your ticket. We must feed the golden ticket machine before we can go any further.'

Eve plucked the ticket from her belt and held it out towards Lester.

'Ah, a green one. Good. It just so happens that his

favourite colour is green.

Buddy sniffed at the rat curiously. Lester pushed a piece of cheese deeper into his waistcoat pocket. He was not sharing his mid-morning snack with anyone, least of all a dog from the human world. Eve bent down and handed the ticket over. Lester snatched it abruptly and immediately posted it through the slot in the front of the golden cylinder. There was a loud gulping noise as the machine swallowed the ticket. It suddenly sprang up on skinny green legs and galloped happily away into the forest. Assuming this was a new game, Buddy gave chase, the bell on his little hat jingling and jangling as he bounced over the brightly coloured toadstools that were dotted amongst the grass and poking through patches of snow.

Eve and Noelle looked around them. The forest was truly wondrous and like nowhere they had ever seen before. Trees towered over them like great leafy skyscrapers, with soft mosses cloaking their roots in vivid neon green. All was quiet but not for long. Suddenly, the peace was broken by a distant howl of anguish and the girls looked at each other in alarm.

'Oh, deary me. Come on.' Lester sighed and scurried off along the pebble path that wound away into the trees. 'We'd better go and see what that's all about.'

Eve shouted for Buddy and, panting from his exertions, he joined the two girls as they hurried after Lester. Not far along the path, in a forest clearing, they found him, hands on hips, staring at a very curious scene.

'What in giddy goodness are you doing, Bow?' Lester asked.

Two little legs were sticking out of a rusty wheelbarrow and kicking furiously as various objects flew from that wheelbarrow onto the path – a bicycle wheel, an old shoe, a flowerpot, and several other items all appeared at some speed. Buddy barked a warning and Eve and Noelle ducked as a small rusty saucepan flew dangerously close. Finally, a head and body emerged from the wheelbarrow and an elf slumped dejectedly to the grass, his back resting against the barrow wheel, skinny legs outstretched.

'This is Bow,' sighed Lester, rolling his eyes. 'Bow *should* be using his magic wheelbarrow to collect the very finest leaves from these Wellness Woods for the Leaf Factory, but it seems to be full of old junk instead.' He poked a toe at the now broken flowerpot. Perrie ignored Lester and fluttered down to the dejected elf. 'Whatever is the matter Bow?' she said kindly.

'Haven't you heard? Eleuia is lost!' wailed Bow miserably. 'And the Star Wish list is nowhere to be found. Oh, Santa is going to need a *very* big bag of cookies before I break the news.' Bow rambled on, shaking his head, and staring at the floor. 'This is terrible timing. Terrible. It's almost the Luna Moon.'

Suddenly, the forest seemed filled with worried voices all talking at once. 'Eleuia is lost?' Eve and Noelle looked at each other and chorused together '*EE-LOO-YA*?' Eve chuckled, testing out the word she had just heard. 'What's that?'.

It was no longer quiet. Elves of all shapes and sizes were emerging from the forest around them and hurrying in all directions. Fairies were fluttering frantically in and out of the trees, chattering and fussing about a lost 'Star wish list' and something called 'Eleuia'. The terrible news was spreading fast.

Eve didn't know what Eleuia was or the Star wish list, but everyone seemed very upset, and she knew what it felt like to lose something precious. Feeling a wave of courage wash over her, Eve took a deep breath and spoke up. 'We'll help you find Eleuia,' she said loudly to no one in particular. Silence fell. Everyone stopped and stared at her, including Noelle, who was surprised by her friend's sudden bold announcement. 'YES!' agreed Noelle. She had no idea what Eve had in mind, but she trusted her best friend, and, in any case, it was sure to be an adventure.

Unseen and overlooked, in the depths of the Wellness Woods, was Gizmo the dragon. Unlike the other inhabitants of the forest, he was delighted to hear that Eleuia was lost. He climbed stealthily up the gigantic willow tree to get a better view of the forest clearing and the brave new elves who seemed determined to help. His scales changed colour as he climbed the trunk. He was perfectly camouflaged as he curled and slithered amongst the branches. He pricked up his ears and peered through the leaves with glittering black eyes. Eve and Noelle were in the centre of a large crowd.

'Hmmmmm,' he growled. 'The race to find Eleuia is on.'

Chapter 6

Where is Eleuia?

Lester was most displeased.

He should be at home by now, in his favourite armchair, nibbling cheese and looking forward to his afternoon snooze. Instead, he had been tasked with leading these human-world strangers and their excitable dog to Mr Arwin's house. Mr Arwin was retired now but he was undoubtedly the wisest elf in the forest and highly respected by the inhabitants of Elfland. Mr Arwin would know what to do.

Lester marched grumpily on ahead, leaving Perrie to answer the avalanche of questions from their visitors. It was a crisp winter's day. Sunlight broke through the woodland canopy and sent shadows dancing across the path that wound its way through the trees. To either side was a rainbow of strange flowers and brightly coloured toadstools and Buddy seemed determined to stop and investigate everyone. Eve and Noelle chattered eagerly to Perrie as she fluttered alongside them, close to their ears.

'So, this lost wish list then...This must be so important to Elfland, we must do everything we can to help you find it. What does it say?' asked Eve, eager to know what all the fuss was about.

'Elves are many things,' Perrie began. 'They're masters in the art of toy making, speedy present-wrappers and bringers of Christmas joy. They work hard to ensure that, every year, Christmas goes smoothly.' She grinned and pirouetted briefly away from them before fluttering back and adopting a more serious tone. 'It is not all about the presents though. Yes, presents are very exciting to receive; no one can deny that. But to have a special wish come true? A wish from the heart? Well, that is something truly wonderful. A Star Wish can make you feel warm and magical inside far longer than any present ever could.'

'Oh, *do* get to the point, Perrie,' grumbled Lester, puffing out his cheeks and slumping onto a nearby toadstool. It was a long walk to Mr Arwin's cottage and, it was fair to say, Lester was *not* in peak physical condition. He released the single brass button of his waistcoat and delved deep into one pocket for the morsel of cheese he had brought along for his mid-morning snack.

Ever ravenous, Buddy sniffed the air and padded towards the grumpy rodent, eager to share in whatever treats might be on offer.

'There is more chance of me turning into Rudolph the reindeer,' Lester snapped, 'than *you* getting any of my cheese.' He abruptly turned his back and began nibbling furiously.

Perrie rolled her eyes and looked pointedly at Eve and Noelle. 'Lester is harmless,' she said loudly. 'But I'm afraid he can be rather *rude* when he's hungry.' She swiped playfully at the bell on the little rodent's hat. It jingled a warning and Lester hunched his shoulders to shield his cheese from further attack.

'Now. Where was I?' wondered Perrie as she fluttered back to the two girls.

'You were telling us about the wish list,' said Noelle.

In the forest, there is an elf named Eleuia,' continued Perrie. 'He is the Wellness Elf. The Wellness Elf's job is a very important one. He makes wishes come true, for children all over the world. The name Eleuia means "wish".'

Realisation dawned on Eve and Noelle. 'So Eleuia is an elf and it's Eleuia who is lost?' they chorused together.

'Exactly!' cried Perrie, buzzing quickly from one to the other. 'All elves know the importance of wellness but there is only one elf with the title of Wellness Elf. The elf is carefully selected to oversee the process of transporting children's Star Wishes down the Dream Stream under the Luna Moon. The spell to activate the magic only works if chanted by the chosen Wellness Elf.' Perrie smiled, thinking of Eleuia. She really did hope he was OK.

'Finally!' muttered Lester, sliding off the toadstool he was perched on. He straightened his waistcoat and, after much huffing and puffing, managed to refasten the little brass button across his large tummy at the second attempt.

'But how does Eleuia make children's wishes come true?' called Eve as Perrie zipped away down the path.

'You'll find out soon enough,' she said over her shoulder. 'Come on!'

I wish...
... to learn how to do a handstand.
... to eat marshmallows toasted on a campfire.
... to hug my mum every day.
... to paint with my grandfather.
... to make lots of friends at my new school.

... for more time to bake with my gran.

... for my friends to be happy.

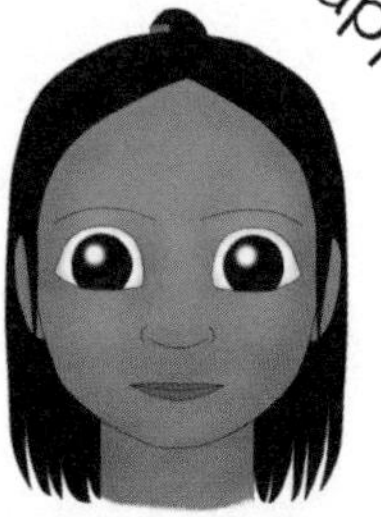

... to learn how to talk to animals, especially my dog!

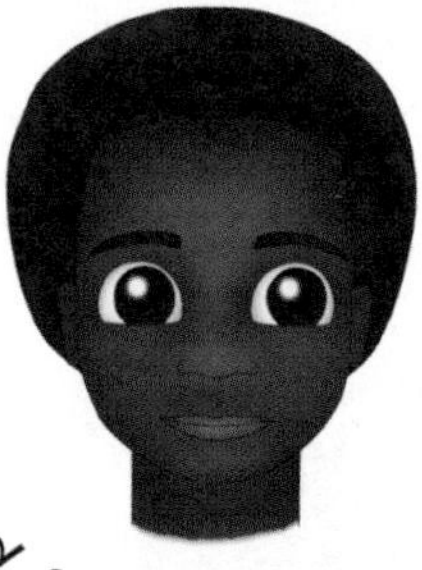

... I could fly to the moon.

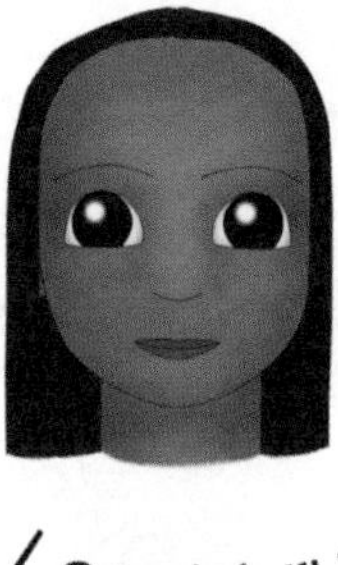

... I could run as fast as a cheetah.

I wish...
... for my family to be happy.
... to see a hedgehog.
... to run faster and score a goal at football.
... to see a real unicorn sparkle.
... that the oceans were plastic free.

... for sunshine and rain so the flowers in my garden bloom.
... for a visit to the beach.
... for my house to be filled with laughter.
... for happiness and good health for all my family.
... I could play all day long.

I wish...
... to become an astronaut when I grow up.
... I could see in the dark.
... for something yummy for tea.
... to swim in the sea with dolphins.
... that I could see a shooting star.

... to stand on top of the tallest mountain.

... to have honey on toast everyday.

... to learn about the stars.

... for today to be a postive day.

... for bright sun to help my little sister's sunflower's grow as tall as her.

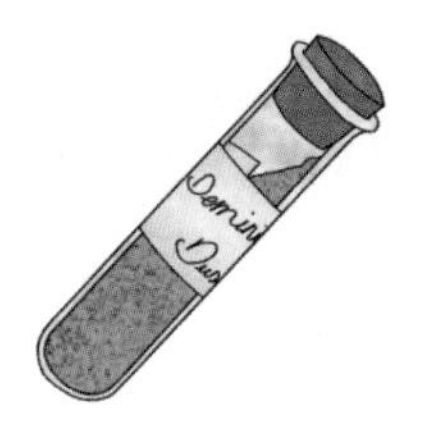

Chapter 7

The Diminishing Dust

They journeyed further into the Wellness Woods, their feet crunching rhythmically on the winding path. Buddy stopped bounding in and out of the undergrowth and loped alongside Eve and Noelle, occasionally pausing to examine a new flower or snap at a buzzing insect. Lester brought up the rear. Tired as he was, he didn't lag too far behind. He became convinced they were being followed and he was sure he had seen movement in the bushes on more than one occasion. Meanwhile, Perrie flickered onward, enthusiastically chattering away and oblivious to Lester's concerns.

Perrie came to a halt beside a tall tree that was somewhat different from the others. Its trunk was smooth and sinuous, and it seemed to shimmer, golden in the rays of the morning sunshine.

Perrie hovered briefly. 'Wait here. I'll just be a moment.' And suddenly, she was away, rocketing straight up into the branches above their heads and disappearing from view.

'Where's she gone?' cried Noelle as they shielded their eyes and peered upwards.

Lester caught them up, puffing heavily. 'Pixie tree,' he gasped, placing his paws on his hips and following Eve and Noelle's gaze. 'She'll be back in a min—'

Sure enough, before he could finish, Perrie was zipping back through the pixie tree leaves, dislodging quite a few as she went. They floated gently to the forest floor as Perrie returned to her expert hovering just a few feet away. She was grinning from ear to ear and holding something new in her hands for Eve and Noelle to inspect.

It was a test tube of some sort. Eve and Noelle had used them in science lessons at school. As they looked more closely, they could see the glass tube had a tiny stopper made of dark brown cork. But what was inside fascinated them the most. Through the glass, they could see movement. A green, sparkling dust seemed to be swirling inside.

Concealed in the trees nearby, Gizmo the dragon pondered this turn of events. He had been silently following that pesky pixie, the miserable Lester, and their strange new friends all morning. He thought Lester may have spotted him once or twice but of course he was far too clever for them.

Why does she need Diminishing Dust? he wondered. *What is she up to?*

He recognised those glittering green swirls instantly. Pixie Diminishing Dust was a magic shrinking potion. Not to be taken lightly and extremely dangerous in the wrong hands. He narrowed his eyes and dipped his head beneath the lowest branch to better hear their conversation.

The girls stared wide-eyed at Perrie's potion but as Eve reached forward, Perrie snatched it away playfully. 'Let's go,' she said, 'we're nearly there!'

Her wings buzzed and she whirled away, leading them deeper into the Wellness Woods.

Chapter 8

A tree trunk doorway

Perrie was right. They were indeed 'nearly there'. With Lester re-energised and leading the way once more, they soon found themselves at their destination.

They came to a halt in front of a remarkable tree that towered regally above all others. Its thick roots snaked away in all directions and its rough trunk, differing from the rest of the wood, was coated in something similar to the fur of a woolly mammoth. It was so enormously wide that Eve and Noelle had no possible chance of holding hands and reaching all the way around it. They would have needed all their classmates to be able to do that. It stretched so high above them that, try as they might, they simply could not see the topmost branches.

They were also unable to see Gizmo. But he *was* there. Above them, hidden amongst the foliage, he coiled over and around a thick branch, looking down at the visitors below. Observing them closely. He knew now where Perrie and Lester had led them. And he suddenly knew what the Diminishing Dust was for.

So dumbfounded had the girls been by the sheer scale of the tree in front of them, they hadn't noticed the very mysterious thing at the base of the gigantic trunk.

'Look at that!' cried Noelle, pointing, and crouching for a closer look. Eve knelt beside her friend. There seemed no end to the magical sights and bizarre events in this strange place.

There, in the giant trunk of the tree, was a small door. The door was arch-shaped, and it was painted blue with a gleaming golden handle that they could just about see their distorted faces reflected in. To one side were two, earthenware pots. They were smothered in moss like the tree trunk itself. Dotted around them, in the shady nooks created by the tree's great roots, a few lingering patches of snow were silently melting. Hanging from a lever to the left of the door there was a thick metal chain with an ornate loop on the end.

'Gosh it's so cute!' cried Noelle excitedly. 'What's that chain for?'

In answer, Lester barged impatiently past the two girls, almost overbalancing Eve in his haste. He leapt awkwardly to grasp the loop at the end of the chain, dangled momentarily and then dropped to the ground. The metal lever dipped and squeaked in protest and somewhere, in the depths of the tree trunk, a bell could faintly be heard. Whoever was inside would be alerted to their presence on the doorstep.

Eve and Noelle looked at each other. Wide-eyed yet again.

'Doorbell!' they said in unison.

Inside, behind the door, slow footsteps were drawing nearer.

Chapter 9

The swirling mist

'We must be quick!' said Perrie, fluttering around them. 'Do exactly as I say. We don't want this to go wrong. Eve? Noelle? Hold hands now. Gather Buddy to you as well.' Eve reached down for Buddy's collar and hauled him in to sit tight against her legs. The girls nervously gripped each other's hands and huddled together, unsure of what was coming next. Satisfied, Perrie spiralled up into the air above the adventurous trio.

As she did so, she popped the little cork and began to scatter the glittering green Diminishing Dust from the tiny test tube. Lester scampered backwards to get out of the way. He was quite happy at the size he was, thank you very much.

Gizmo watched from his perch high in the tree and knew he had to act. Swiftly, he slithered, unseen, from his hiding place and down to the very base of the tree. There, concealed behind one of the great tree's largest roots and only a few feet away from Eve and Noelle, he waited for his chance.

As Perrie pirouetted and twirled above them, the sparkling dust began to shower over Eve and Noelle.

They screwed their eyes tight shut and tried not to breathe. Buddy snorted and sneezed as the glittering particles enveloped him and puffs of green smoke and white stars exploded around the children in a magical mini fireworks display.

With the pixie occupied, and Lester momentarily distracted by the magic, Gizmo the dragon seized his chance. Unfurling his long tail, he caught a good deal of the dust for himself before it tumbled to the forest floor and vanished. Too much dust, actually. Gizmo wasn't aware there was an art to delivering Diminishing Dust.

It was a skill Perrie had practised to perfection.

Amid the swirling mist and within just a few seconds, Eve, Noelle, and Buddy began to shrink. So too did the dragon.

Down they went.

Smaller... And smaller... And smaller.

As the green smoke cleared and the last of the white stars popped, fizzed, and crackled, the children slowly opened their eyes. Confused for a moment, Buddy quickly recovered and seemed delighted to find himself the same size as Lester. Lester was less impressed with this turn of events and was soon fending off frighteningly exuberant Buddy-licks.

The girls paid little heed to Lester's battle with Buddy. They were still facing the spot where the small blue door had been, but it suddenly seemed much, much larger. Where once they had had to kneel for a closer look, the door now loomed above them. They could easily pick out the grain of the wood from which it was made and the earthenware pots on either side reached as high as the thick black belts of their Elfland outfits.

'Goodness. That magic dust has made everything much much bigger, hasn't it!' exclaimed Noelle.

'It's not everything else that's got bigger! It's us!' cried Eve. '*We've* got smaller!'

'Gosh, if we had a set of wings each, we'd be pixies, just like Perrie.' Noelle giggled, twirling around.

Perrie had settled on the doorstep and folded her wings. She was smiling mischievously at the two girls. *She's much taller than before,* thought Eve. Then she shook her head quickly and reminded herself it was the other way round. *They* were smaller. She could see much more of the detail in Perrie's wings and the embroidery of her flowing red pixie dress. It was truly beautiful.

Hidden behind the earthenware pot to the left of the door sat Gizmo. He too had shrunk to a fraction of his former size.

Having unknowingly caught too much Diminishing Dust, he was now no bigger than a large, exotic caterpillar and his wings were almost unrecognisable, folded as they were against his body. He didn't like being this small and insignificant. He was used to towering over others with his size and strength. But needs must.

They were all distracted from their thoughts by the very definite sounds of a key rattling in a lock and metal bolts sliding back. Eve squeezed Noelle's hand and looked at the door. Perrie fluttered lightly from the doorstep, and she too turned to face the door. Lester, who was quickly learning how to manage a bouncing Buddy, grabbed him by the collar and stood to attention.

Creaking loudly on ancient hinges, the door opened.

Chapter 10

Gizmo sneaks inside

Behind the door, in the shadows of the hallway, stood a hooded figure. Nervously, Eve and Noelle took a half step backwards as Buddy gave a low growl of warning.

'Greetings, Eve and Noelle. I've been expecting you,' said a kindly voice.

The owner of the voice stepped into the pool of sunlight that illuminated the threshold. His weathered hands reached to the blue hood that still hid his face and dropped it to his shoulders.

The girls gasped. 'It's you!'

Beaming back at them was the curious little man from the Christmas market. Though, now that the children had been sprinkled with Diminishing Dust, he was taller than them! His familiar blue eyes sparkled from his weathered, wrinkled face and his snow-white beard flowed all the way to his waist.

Mr Arwin chuckled, noticing the confusion on their faces. The girls were momentarily rooted to the spot, but Buddy trotted forward to nuzzle the man's hand. Mr Arwin ruffled behind Buddy's ear, and he sat down immediately, tail thudding happily on the doorstep. Lester and Perrie stood at a respectful distance. They too were amused by Eve and Noelle's open-mouthed shock.

Watching from a dark corner behind one of the pots, Gizmo was waiting for his moment – his tiny head now bright pink. He was extremely embarrassed, being this small instead of his usual mighty self.

Mr Arwin smiled again. 'Now then, young ladies. I realise this must have been a most surprising day but if you're not careful, you're going to start catching flies!' The girls abruptly closed their mouths. 'You'll be needing some magic if you're to continue on your quest.'

He pointed one wizened finger at Eve's belt. She looked down. In the wide black belt where she had tucked the plain wooden spoon, there was now something quite different. She pulled it from the belt and held it up. It was certainly still wooden, but it was far more interesting than a plain old spoon. It was an Elfland Wish Wand. Carved into the handle were intricate designs and strange lettering and, atop it, there was a five-pronged star. As she turned it over in her hands, Eve noticed that on one side of the star was written her elf name: *Eve*. And on the other was carved one simple word: *Wish*.

'Let's charge that Wish Wand, shall we?' Mr Arwin said, beckoning them in with that same wizened finger and Eve and Noelle hurried forward with Lester and Perrie not far behind. Buddy, bold and brave as ever, led them all inside and the door began to swing shut.

Gizmo leapt from his hiding place. He hated being so small and insignificant, but it served his purpose... for now. He raced for the rapidly closing door, claws skittering across the stone step. He had to get inside Mr Arwin's cottage. The door kept moving. The gap, and the opportunity, were disappearing, fast. He galloped hard and made a desperate dive for the door. He slid through headfirst, on his scaly tummy, just managing to pull in his tail as the lock clicked shut behind him. He had done it. Gizmo was inside and no one had noticed.

Chapter 11

The charging of the wand

Inside, lanterns were hanging everywhere – just like at the market stall. The candlelight cast a warm and friendly glow and sent mischievous shadows dancing into every corner of the room.

A comforting fragrance of cinnamon and pine brought memories of the Christmas market. *Gosh,* thought Noelle, *that seems so long ago.*

The girls stood still and turned slowly, taking in the scene. Under their feet was a thick, richly patterned carpet that enveloped their elf slippers. Despite being inside the tree, above their heads was a night sky that seemed littered with stars, stretching as far as they could see. Around the edges of the room – and half-hidden in the shadows – cupboards, shelves, caskets, and sea-chests were groaning under the weight of mysterious jars, ornate boxes, ribbon-wrapped scrolls, and all manner of strange artefacts. Buddy had already set off to investigate. He was patrolling the perimeter, sniffing at everything curiously. Perrie and Lester, who had both been here many times before, had already helped themselves to a wooden stool each. Perrie sat cross-legged, absent-mindedly inspecting her nails whilst Lester rummaged in his pockets for one more crumb of cheese. He was hungry... again.

In the very centre of the room was a huge oval table. It was astonishingly beautiful and made from one piece of timber just like the one at the Christmas market. The tabletop, much like the market stall, was almost obscured by a range of small treasures and fascinating objects.

Mr Arwin seemed to be searching for something.

'Come. Come,' he implored them over his shoulder. 'Come and sit down.'

The girls looked at each other and moved towards the table.

'Where did I put it?' Mr Arwin muttered, picking through the items on the table.

'You said something about charging this?' Eve reminded him, holding out the wand.

'Ah yes,' he said, turning his attention to her. He took the wand in both hands and held it up, balanced on his palms. The girls watched expectantly.

He began to chant softly in an odd language that Eve and Noelle had never heard before. They sat together in French at school. And this *wasn't* French. Mr Arwin closed his eyes slowly and continued his strange mumbling and muttering. To their surprise, the wand suddenly began to rise from his hands. It lifted off just a few centimetres and, as Mr Arwin spoke, it began to spin. Faster and faster, it went, like the blades of a helicopter. Within a few seconds it was just a blur. Then, as quickly as it had begun, it was over. Mr Arwin opened his eyes, the wand came to an abrupt halt and dropped back into his outstretched hands.

'There,' he said, 'all done!' Once again distracted by his table, he returned the wand to Eve and continued his search. She stared at it, unsure of what she had just witnessed.

'That is no longer just a pretty piece of wood,' Mr Arwin said, inspecting a small music box before replacing it on the table. 'Your wand is now fully charged, and it has the most wonderful powers. With that wand of yours, you can grant people all sorts of wishes and emotions such as happiness, courage, patience, kindness, confidence, strength, or laughter.

He waved his hand in their general direction as he

spoke, though his attention was focused on the table in front of him.

Not for the first time that day, Eve, and Noelle stared at each other in wonder.

'Ah! Here it is!' Mr Arwin exclaimed, holding aloft a small brass box. He appeared to have found the item he had been searching for. He lifted the lid and plucked a tiny piece of paper from within. It was about the size of a postage stamp. Eve and Noelle stepped closer to him for a better view.

He cleared a space on the table and quickly scooped a handful of glittering growth dust from a bowl. He scattered it across the fragment of paper and recited a simple chant.

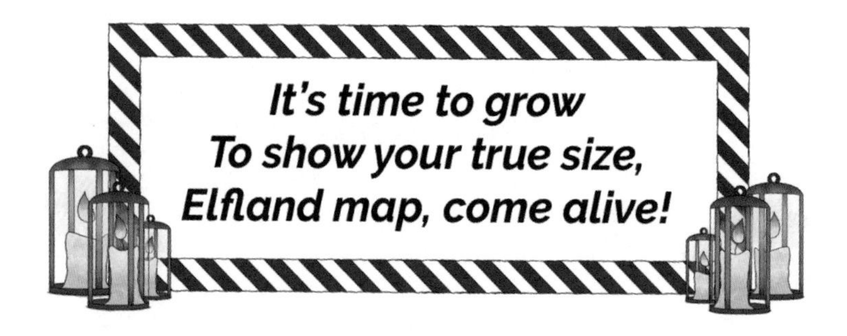

There was a sudden explosion of sparks. Eve and Noelle had to shield their eyes.

When they opened them, where the postage-stamp-sized piece of paper had been was a large scroll of paper which, Mr Arwin, was busy pinning flat with various objects he plucked from the table.

'For you,' he said with a flourish.

ELfLand
N
W
E
S
Stinky Swamp
Elfland Adventures
Sensory Retreats Elf Care
Rory Star
Astaria Entrance
Believe Bridge
Sweet Treats Café
Sorting Office
Floating Stepping Stones
Enchanted Forest
Wellness Woods
Mr Arwin's House
Leaf Factory
Santa's Grotto
Perrie's Pixie Garden
Elfland Entrance
Here be dragons!

Chapter 12

A map to guide the way

It was a map.

The scroll was full of detail. There were beautiful drawings and strange place names, and the girls spent some moments peering at it.

'It's Elfland,' Eve said excitedly. Noelle squeezed in next to her, tracing a finger over the Wellness Woods. The girls scanned the map together. They could see the path they had taken that morning with Lester and Perrie.

'Sweet Treats Café?' Noelle read happily. 'We MUST visit Sweet Treats Café.' Her mouth started to water. 'And look! A Leaf Factory? That sounds good.'

Eve was thoughtful. She hadn't forgotten the important task they had volunteered for. They had to find Eleuia and the missing Star Wish list. She glanced up at Mr Arwin.

'Do *you* know where Eleuia is?' she asked. 'What does he look like?'

'Yes. And what is the Luna Moon?' asked Noelle. 'How does Eleuia make the wishes come true? And can we go to the Sweet Treats Café?'

'What a beautiful name – As-ta-ria. Astaria Entrance,' read Eve, pointing to the writing next to a rainbow. 'What is Astaria?' she asked.

Mr Arwin looked from one to the other. 'So many questions.' He chuckled. 'Let me see if I can answer them.' He settled himself into one of the six golden chairs around the table.

In the shadows by the door, where he had been crouching silently, Gizmo narrowed his black eyes and pricked up his ears. If anyone knew the whereabouts of Eleuia, Gizmo needed to find out. He must get there first.

'Astaria is our home. It is home to many elves and magical creatures, a land where unicorns fly and dragons soar, living in harmony. Home to the finest elf academy. It is the academy that carefully selects elves to come to Elfland. It is an honour to be chosen,' Mr Arwin explained.

'Astaria sounds amazing!' said Eve.

'Yes, it is quite spectacular. But you can only go to and from Astaria under the Luna Moon when the portal opens, within the rainbow arch. Only those selected by the academy's Enchantress, by Santa or by the Wellness Elf are allowed to pass through.' Mr Arwin sighed.

'I was once the Wellness Elf myself,' he said. 'Long before you two were born and many years before Eleuia took over. It is a great honour to be a Wellness Elf. Eleuia was in training for many moons – he's a natural! If Eleuia is not found soon, then a great many children's Star Wishes will go unanswered. You see, it's the Wellness Elf's job to listen to those wishes, to look after them, and to deliver them safely down the Dream Stream that flows through the Elfland forest.'

He paused and noticed the confused looks that Eve and Noelle gave each other. It was a lot to take in, certainly.

'But how does it all work and why is Eleuia so important? Can't somebody else do the job?' asked Eve.

'It is a simple, but important, process,' replied Mr Arwin patiently. 'Let me explain. Firstly, the wishes of children from all over the world arrive at the Elfland Sorting Office. From there, the Wellness Elf or one of his trusted apprentices must collect them and deliver them to the Leaf Factory. There, an army of elves, scribe them onto beautiful leaves. Letterboxes, rather like the one you probably encountered at the gates to Elfland, transport the leaves with the children's wishes to the Believe Bridge where the Wellness Elf sends them on their way, bobbing down the Dream Stream. It is quite magnificent – they go through the rainbow arch under the light of the Rory Star and explode into a million twinkling diamonds of possibilities. That bit is perhaps the most important. It is vital that the wishes drift away by the light of the Luna Moon or there is no chance of them ever coming true.'

'Gosh.' Eve sighed. 'It doesn't *sound* like a very simple process to me.'

'And does every wish come true?' asked Noelle.

'Most of the time,' explained Mr Arwin. 'It is the job of the Wellness Elf to check them. You see, some wishes don't come true as it may not be in the best interests of the child. Sometimes wishes don't come true because something far better is on its way. It can also take time. Wishes would come true at an appropriate time and that may be at some point in the distant future. We don't always get what we want immediately. That wouldn't be right at all.'

Mr Arwin sat back in his chair and clicked his fingers. A blue-and-white China tea set clattered and tumbled from a wooden dresser at one side of the room. Cups and saucers danced across the table as a matching teapot poured warm berry tea.

Eve and Noelle were starting to take these sorts of fantastical events for granted. It had been one of those days! Besides, they suddenly found themselves very thirsty and very hungry after all the talk of a Sweet Treats Café. Querying yet another astonishing event would have been wasted time.

As if reading their minds, Mr Arwin clicked his fingers once more and, from the opposite corner of the room, a huge platter of delicious-looking nutritious treats flew towards them. Brightly coloured berries circled around what looked like tiny, peeled oranges. The sweetest fruit was spread before them. And a huge chocolate cake too!

'Eve and Noelle have a lot to learn,' said Perrie, stepping up to the table to take a cup of berry tea. She winked at Mr Arwin.

Lester, who had dozed off, was suddenly wide awake, nose twitching. He could smell cake. He sat up, straightened his hat and made for the source of that delicious smell. 'Unfortunately, there is only one Luna Moon each month, and it's tonight, the most important moon of the month!' he told them as he reached out a paw for the largest slice he could find.

'Tonight?!' Eve spluttered into her tea.

'Panic not!' Mr Arwin reassured her. 'You have

plenty of time. Assuming, of course, that Eleuia can be found.'

'That's alright then,' said Noelle, eagerly reaching for another orange.

'I'd panic if I were you,' muttered Lester through a mouthful of crumbs.

'Lester!' Mr Arwin warned. 'I'm relying on you to look after Eve and Noelle and to help guide them on their journey. *Do* try to be a little more positive!' Lester reluctantly nodded in agreement, shrugged, and took another enormous bite of delicious chocolate cake.

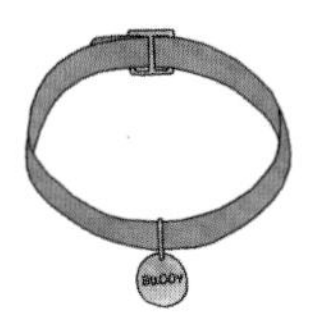

Chapter 13

The tiny stowaway

With Lester contentedly rubbing his tummy, it was time for them all to leave. Still lurking in the shadows, Gizmo was more impatient and irritated than he had ever been. He had endured the sight of them all glugging berry tea and wolfing down the sweetest fruit and he was ravenously hungry now. He feared that his rumbling stomach might give him away. He shrank deeper into the shadows as Mr Arwin showed his visitors to the door.

Outside, Perrie pirouetted above the girls once more and sprinkled them with the Growth Glitter that Mr Arwin had given them. It showered from the test tube, and, in a puff of smoke and a crackle of stars, the girls and Buddy were returned to their original size.

Mr Arwin shooed Lester out onto the doorstep.

'Quick, out you go Lester,' he ordered. 'You must get back to your guiding duties!' Lester's ears drooped at this sad news. He waddled miserably out into the winter sunshine and joined the others. Lester was already weary, and he longed for a visit from Remi, the telepathic, teleporting Sleepy Elf. He'd happily admit that Remi was the best elf he'd encountered since arriving in Elfland all those years ago.

The Sleepy Elf's mesmerising voice ensured all who listened had the most restful night's sleep. Lester wished he was lying on a hammock listening to the Sleepy Elf's guided meditation instead of traipsing off on an adventure he had not volunteered for!

Unnoticed, Gizmo crept out from behind the door and sneaked back behind the same earthenware pot where he had hidden previously. He was kicking himself now. He'd missed his chance to grab some of that Growth Glitter. He was stuck at this small and insignificant size. He sulked, knowing he would have to wait for the Diminishing Dust to wear off and that it could take a fair few hour! He was used to being a powerful dragon with a roar that struck fear into the hearts of every elf, not some snivelling little caterpillar with a weedy voice that no one could hear.

The last tendrils of the Growth Glitter smoke were starting to clear and curl away as Eve and Noelle hugged tightly, relieved to be back to their original size. Gizmo had a decision to make, and he had to make it fast. He couldn't let Eve and Noelle out of his sight for they were the ones who would lead him to Eleuia.

Under cover of the low-lying green smoke, he charged from his hiding place and leapt. Buddy barked suddenly and began turning in frantic circles, chasing his tail. Eve and Noelle laughed.

'You crazy dog.' Eve chuckled, grabbing him by the collar and ruffling his ears. 'Is it nice to be back to your normal size?'

Hidden in Buddy's thick coat and perilously close to his bottom, Gizmo was most unhappy. He'd had only one option and that was to conceal himself on the human's pet.

'Grizzling goblins,' Gizmo growled to himself. 'I will never live this down.'

'Good boy, Buddy.' Eve snuggled her friend and calmed him. She looked to Mr Arwin for their next instruction. Gizmo, meanwhile, picked his way stealthily across the dog's back. He clambered through the thick, rust-brown fur and found himself a safe spot on Buddy's collar. Here, he could travel with them unseen. He dug in with sharp claws and held on tight.

'Drat! It's going to be a bumpy ride,' he moaned to himself. 'I'll never go near that Diminishing Dust again.'

'Now then. Off you go,' said Mr Arwin. 'Perrie? Lester? I think you should lead our friends here...' Mr Arwin pointed to a candy-cane-shaped building on the map, labelled Sorting Office. 'That seems to me to be a good place to start.'

Perrie and Lester gave an extravagant salute and, with the girls in tow waving goodbye, they set off once more.

Chapter 14

The Sorting Office

Sometime later, the adventurers stepped out of the trees and into a clearing. The early afternoon sun was shining down from an ice-blue sky, melting the few remaining patches of snow. Buddy dropped to roll in a puddle of muddy water, and this woke a dozing Gizmo. The Diminishing Dust was sure to wear off soon and, with the dog distracted, Gizmo slithered from Buddy's collar and scurried to the toe of Eve's elf slipper before anyone could notice.

Buddy leapt back onto his four paws and shook himself furiously. Great splats of mud sprayed in all directions.

Eve and Noelle shielded themselves and Perrie quickly fluttered out of range.

'Buddy!' shouted Eve. 'Stop!'

Lester wiped a splatter of sticky mud from the end of his snout. 'Yuck!'

It had been a brief and unwelcome distraction from the incredible building that stood before them.

'Here we are!' cried Perrie triumphantly. 'The Sorting Office. This is where the Star Wishes arrive and where Eleuia *should* be right now.'

Noelle stared at the red-and-white-striped structure in front of them. Shaped like an upright candy cane with small turrets on either side, the Sorting Office was really quite spectacular and like no building they had ever seen. Before they had time to admire it further or even enjoy the sugary-sweet smells that seemed to be wafting from its windows, a large door in the centre of one wall burst open with a loud bang. They were all startled as an elf, the girls had not yet come across, came racing merrily out of the doorway. His elf hat was perched precariously on a shock of curly black hair, and he had a big welcoming grin.

'Hello, bonjour, ciao, hallo, buenos diazzzzzz, my friends!' he shouted cheerily. Arms flung wide, he hopped and skipped down the grassy slope to greet them.

'Bing!' Perrie flew over, excited to see the Chief of Communications. She loved the Sorting Office. It was a hugely important building in Elfland, and Bing was in charge of it all.

'Bing is soooo clever!' she explained. 'He can speak multiple languages and is responsible for collecting children's Star Wishes from all over the world.' She fizzed past Eve and Noelle and danced happily around Bing's head. She had quite the soft spot for Bing. He had the most beautiful twinkling eyes, she thought.

'Overrated I'd say,' grumbled Lester, folding his arms, and scuffing a toe in the dirt.

Bing blushed at Perrie's high praise and turned to Eve and Noelle. 'Welcome, everyone. Come along inside. I thought you might be visiting today.' He signalled for everyone to follow him through the door and into the Sorting Office reception area. 'We heard a rumour that Eleuia was missing and had hoped it wasn't true. Eleuia collected the Star Wish list this morning and the Luna Moon is tonight. He must be found!' He rubbed his forehead wearily. There was a whole month's worth of children's Star wishes on that list.

Clinging to Eve's elf slipper, Gizmo listened intently to this new information.

So, Eleuia has already collected the list. I must find it before them and destroy it – the children's wishes must NOT go down the Dream Stream. If my wish for friendship can't come true, then nobody's will!

'Follow me.' Bing led them through another door. Gizmo grabbed his chance and clambered from his hiding place on Eve's slipper. His scales were starting to itch, and he knew the power of the Diminishing Dust was starting to wane. Small as he still was, he managed to slip underneath a nearby cupboard door and he just caught a glimpse of Lester hurrying after the others, his little bottom wiggling through the reception door as it closed behind them.

Gizmo turned to look at the cupboard he had chosen for his new hiding place. There was a bucket, a broom and what looked like a mop propped in one corner. Steady drips of water fell from its threads. It had been used recently.

'A cleaning cupboard? What an indignity!' raged Gizmo. It was bad enough that he had been forced to travel on the filthy collar of a smelly old dog. And now, here he was having to cower in a cleaning cupboard. They would pay for this!

'I'll be ready for them on the way out,' he snarled.

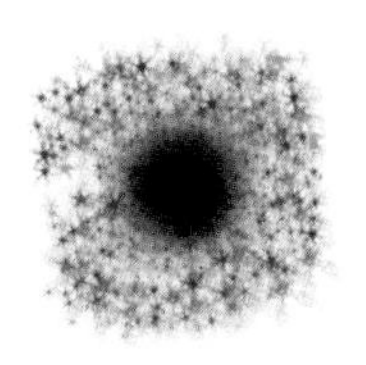

Chapter 15

Magic grinds to a halt

Eve and Noelle were completely mesmerised as Bing led them onto the floor of the brightly lit Sorting Office. A spiralling wooden staircase snaked around all four walls of the vast hall. Above their heads, where a solid ceiling should have been, there was a gigantic swirling portal. Sheets of paper in all shapes, sizes and colours were emerging through it and fluttering down through the air. They were children's wishes of many types and all made with good intentions for themselves or their loved ones. Some were written down; some were whispered aloud, and some were yearned for silently whilst gazing at the stars, but they all arrived here at the Elfland Sorting Office. Now, they flapped and flickered and snapped and danced, magically organising themselves into an alphabetical filing system that stretched down the great hall and as far as the eye could see. Merry music was playing loudly, and the letters and notes seemed to be dancing in time. It was an infectious beat and even Lester couldn't resist. He lifted up a paw to tap along and, without realising, started wagging his furry bottom from left to right.

'Cool moves!' called an elf, skipping down the stairs towards them. Lester stopped immediately, turning a bright shade of pink. The only time he normally danced was when eating cheese. And he certainly didn't see any cheese around here. He wasn't sure what had come over him.

'Welcome to the Sorting Office,' said the new elf cheerily. She nodded at Eve, Noelle, and Perrie. 'You too, *Disco Diva*!' she chuckled, winking at Lester. He blushed a deeper shade of scarlet and shuffled his feet. 'And you, handsome boy,' she said, snuggling her face into Buddy's neck and giving him a hug. She clearly loved dogs so Eve knew they would get along.

Noelle interrupted proceedings to compliment the elf's hairstyle. 'Your hair is so cool!' she said enviously, admiring the elf's braids that had been twisted into two rather impressive buns on either side of her head. Unlike Bing, this elf's hat sat straight and true on her head.

'Thank you!' She smiled. 'It takes ages to do in the mornings.'

Perrie made the introductions.

'This is Tinsel. Bing's twin sister. She's a Sensory Elf. Tinsel can sense how we really feel about things and tell when we're putting on a brave face,' Perrie said. Eve and Noelle tilted their heads. They weren't sure about this. 'One Christmas, I was gifted a new orange dress and I smiled happily and said I loved it,' continued Perrie. 'But Tinsel here, sensed I was disappointed.' Perrie laughed.

'And it was true, I *was* quite dismayed. I thought I looked like a tiny orange.'

'It's so lovely to meet you both,' said Eve, looking at the clever twin elves. 'I'm really sorry Eleuia is lost. We're trying our best to help find your Wellness Elf. I was wondering if—'

Before she could finish, the lights in the Sorting Office Hall began to flicker. There was a grinding of gears and a loud clunking noise. Everyone looked up. The rotation of the great portal above their heads had slowed and with a final, wheezy pop, it stopped turning completely. The music stopped too, and the room fell silent but for the fluttering of a thousand letters as they drifted lifelessly to the floor like confetti. No longer dancing. No longer magically filing themselves away ready for transport to the Leaf Factory.

'Oh, my goodness! Oh NO!' cried Bing in a fluster. 'This can't be happening.' He peered upward at the portal. It was receding. Shrinking back. Getting smaller and smaller.

'What's happening?' asked Eve. She could sense that something was very wrong, and she didn't need Tinsel's special powers to tell her.

Lester too was alarmed. He tried to explain.

'Eleuia is Elfland's Wellness Elf. Apart from everything else, it is he who keeps the wellness magic charged, like a battery. No Wellness Elf means *no* wellness magic, *no* Sorting Office, and *no* flowing Dream

Stream. This is bad!'

Amidst the rising panic, Tinsel smiled reassuringly at Lester. Lester always acted as if he cared about nothing but cheese and snoozing, but Tinsel knew that, deep down, he cared a great deal about a lot of things.

'Eleuia left here earlier today and was heading for the Sweet Treats Café,' Tinsel said, looking at Eve, who could sense her strength and determination. 'Follow the trail there.' Turning to her twin brother, she said, 'We will need to start filing these letters the old-fashioned way.' She began gathering notes from the floor.

Sweet Treats Café? Noelle thought, excited at the possibility of a tasty snack. Then she felt instantly guilty for thinking about biscuits at a time of great peril in the Sorting Office. Tinsel gave her a wink and whispered, 'Try the Ginger Snap Special, it's mouth-wateringly good.'

They said their farewells and Perrie led them from the Sorting Office Hall, zooming ahead on silvery wings that became just a blur of buzzing movement. Lester hustled along to the rear, and they all hurried back through the reception area and straight past the cleaning cupboard. The cupboard where Gizmo the dragon was growing larger and larger and suddenly finding his latest hiding place, a bit of a tight squeeze.

Chapter 16

Lester surges ahead

Perrie led them west to the Sweet Treats Café. It seemed the logical thing to do since the last sightings of Eleuia were reported there. For the moment, they all agreed it would be best to keep it a secret that Elfland Sorting Office operations had come to a grinding halt.

'All the elves in these woods play some part in ensuring children's wishes come true,' whispered Perrie. 'If they think there's a chance that those wishes won't flow along the Dream Stream tonight, there'll be uproar!' Eve and Noelle nodded their understanding.

'We can't have all the elves running around the forest in a panic,' puffed Lester as he hurried alongside, trying to keep up with the others. 'There will be chaos and—' He stopped talking. His nose was twitching.

Delicious smells of sweet strawberries were drifting on the air in this part of the Wellness Woods. He licked his lips and urged his little legs onwards.

'Nearly there!' he called, surging ahead of the others.

As they rounded a corner, the Sweet Treats Café came into view, emerging from behind one of the larger woodland trees. It was an impressive sight. Less impressive was Lester, who they found spreadeagled on a moss-covered rock, trying to catch his breath.

Whilst Perrie flapped her wings to cool Lester's sweaty brow, Eve and Noelle forgot about their urgent mission and joined Buddy in his bouncy excitement. This place was the stuff of dreams!

They were standing outside what appeared to be a gigantic toadstool. It was just like the ones they had seen in all those fairy tale picture books, with a fat stem and a scarlet dome with large white polka dots. From the domed roof, on silver chains, there hung a large and beautifully painted wooden sign: 'SWEET TREATS CAFÉ'.

And through the open door beneath, the girls could see a wide staircase snaking up into the interior. Here and there, in the circular walls of the toadstool, there were small casement windows adorned with cheery yellow curtains.

And the smells! Oh, the sweet smells emerging from that café and enveloping them were the most delicious that Eve and Noelle had ever known. From inside, they could hear the noise of contented chatter and the rattle of teacups on saucers. It looked *and* sounded like a wonderfully friendly place.

'We need to get in there and find out where Eleuia was heading off to when he left the café,' said Eve, regaining some composure and bringing everyone's attention back to the task at hand.

'Let's go and talk to Cookie,' said Perrie, fluttering away towards the entrance.

'We're going to talk to a biscuit?' cried Noelle. She was astonished. This day was getting stranger by the second.

Lester sat up, slid off the rock and rolled his eyes.

'Cookie is *not* a biscuit.' He sighed. 'She's a cat! We don't always get on... for *obvious* reasons,' he said, gesturing to himself.

'It's not because you're a rat,' said Perrie. 'It's because you're always playing tricks on her, you naughty rascal.' She looked pointedly at the little round rodent.

'Well anyway,' said Lester, waving away Perrie's correction. 'Cookie owns this establishment. She is assisted by an elf called Pretzel who, I have to say, is one of the most annoyingly happy elves you are ever likely to meet.'

The girls and Buddy followed Perrie to the bottom of the staircase, where they waited for a group of elves to exit. There were twelve in the group, all dressed similarly to Eve and Noelle. They were chatting happily and munching on cookies as they went, and each one paused to say thank you and to wish Eve and Noelle a cheery 'Good day!'

The Eleuia hunters climbed the café stairs.

Chapter 17

Sweet treats for everyone

At the top of the stairs, they were met with the sight of a busy café doing a brisk trade. Rickety wooden tables and chairs filled the space. So tightly packed were they, that Eve and Noelle had to turn sideways to shuffle between them on their way to the counter. At each table, there were groups of elves chatting and laughing. They politely pulled in their chairs as the girls squeezed by. Every table seemed to be groaning under the weight of wonderful cakes, delicious cookies, and fruit platters. And each contented customer was sipping warm berry tea from a China cup.

From the walls, at all sorts of jaunty angles, hung photos of Elfland, old and new. They were arranged and displayed in a variety of heavily carved picture frames. There were pictures of Santa on his sleigh, elves in the workshop, a photo of Tinsel and Bing standing proudly outside the Sorting Office, and many more of elves they had not yet met on their adventure. Eve diverted to look closely at a large photo of a beautiful bridge that arched over a stream.

'That's the Believe Bridge,' Perrie informed her as she fluttered next to her shoulder. 'You can just see the leaves with the wishes floating down the Dream Stream.'

So busy was the café, that nobody paid any heed to the soft thud of a dragon landing on the roof and the scrabbling scratch of claws as he fought for his balance.

Gizmo was back. Back to his normal size and back on the trail of Eve and Noelle. The effects of the Diminishing Dust had run their course and, having extricated himself unseen from the Sorting Office, he had raced to catch up with the children and their Elfland guides. He slid across the roof, dug his claws into the guttering and lowered one glittering black eye to a window. There on the counter, he spied a stack of Cookie's famous honey and banana biscuits in a large glass jar. His tummy gave a hungry growl. How he longed for some of those delicious treats. Turning his attention to the room, he noticed that every table was occupied with elves laughing merrily with their family and friends. How he longed for friends too, to share some of that wonderful warmth and happiness. Quickly, though, he discarded that wish once more. He was a strong and powerful dragon, and he didn't need... anyone!

'Pretzel!' Arms outstretched, Perrie flickered rapidly across the room to the café counter where Cookie's assistant was humming happily to himself and absent-mindedly scooping ice cream into chocolate-dipped cones. He popped the last snow cone into a holder and turned to Perrie with wide, excited eyes. They seemed to know each other well for they began the most hilarious, happy little jig – a dance routine that looked like it had been practised before, though *not* very successfully. Pretzel was all arms and crazy legs. In trying to mirror Perrie's graceful kicks and pirouettes, he almost sent a jar of treacle and blueberry cookies crashing to the floor.

'Whoops!' He laughed, brushing thick dark hair from his eyes. 'That was close!' Pretzel was very tall for an elf and his gangly limbs probably didn't suit the cramped space behind the counter, especially when there was dancing to be done. He moved the jar to safety and shouted over his shoulder in the direction of the kitchen.

'Cookie! Look who's here!'

Lester gulped and shuffled behind Noelle's left leg. The last time he'd seen Cookie, she had been trying to remove the hat that Lester had glued to her head with a dollop of jam.

Out through the kitchen's saloon-style doors bustled Cookie the cat – pastry chef extraordinaire and proprietor of the Sweet Treats Café. She had a jolly, welcoming face and a broad grin for her new customers. She was wearing a custard-splodged apron, tightly knotted around her waist and she was stirring something delicious in a mixing bowl that was tucked in the crook of her right paw. On her head, she had a tall white chef's hat with what looked like a light dusting of pink icing sugar.

A new hat thought Lester guiltily, as he peered from behind Noelle's legs. *The other one was covered in jam; I seem to remember.*

'Welcome! Welcome!' Cookie said kindly, acknowledging the two girls and nodding at Perrie. 'Let me find you a table. Pretzel will bring you some tea and cake.'

Ignoring their rumbling tummies and the delicious smells from the kitchen, Eve and Noelle politely refused Cookie's offer and quickly explained the reason for their visit.

'You see, we really must find Eleuia before it's too late. And we heard that this is where he was last seen,' explained Eve earnestly.

'He certainly was here earlier today but I don't—' Cookie stopped suddenly. Her whiskers bristled and her eyes narrowed. 'Is that a rascally rat I smell?'

Outside on the roof, Gizmo grinned, revealing sharp teeth. 'Oh. This will be *very* entertaining,' he chuckled. He very much enjoyed observing the discomfort of others and Lester probably deserved whatever was about to come his way.

Chapter 18

Snoreberries

Cookie greeted Lester with extended claws and a furious pounce.

The dining area was in instant uproar. Cookie and Lester slithered, skittered, twisted and turned, thudding into table legs and knocking over chairs. Teacups went tumbling and crashing to the floor as the elves jumped up to avoid the trouble. Eve and Noelle watched in slow-motion horror as the bowl of ice cream that Pretzel had been using to make the snow cones flew in an arc through the air and landed – PLOP! – upside down on a customer's head. The terrified rodent

was scurrying as fast as his little paws would carry him to escape the clutches of the angry cat. He decided that, if he survived this, he would stop the pranks forever. Or at least for the next few Luna Moons.

'ENOUGH!' commanded Eve, stamping her elf slipper and shaking her head furiously. 'We need to find Eleuia. We don't have time for this!' Cookie and Lester came to a screeching halt. Panting hard, Lester slumped to the floor. A blob of ice cream slipped slowly from his hat, down his nose and into his lap. Cookie, who was not in the best of shape either, was trying to recover her composure. She straightened her tea-soaked apron and shot daggers at the naughty rodent. Her relieved customers began to put the chairs back on their feet, picking up crockery and returning to their table conversations.

'Shall we start again?' asked Eve. She raised her eyebrows at the two bedraggled creatures in front of her. Cookie and Lester stared guiltily at the floor. 'My name's Eve and it's very nice to meet you, Cookie. Your café is quite spectacular.' Eve could see that Cookie was embarrassed at all the fuss *and* the mess and she was keen to make peace and lift Cookie's spirits. The café certainly *was* spectacular. There was a large Christmas tree in the corner that had survived the chase (just) and it was adorned with candy canes of all shapes, sizes and colours. The counter displayed rows and rows of the café's famous ice cream flavours and there were piles of cookies and muffins on grand golden cake stands and silver platters. Noelle's mouth was watering.

Never one to dwell on an argument, Pretzel began humming again and went to fetch a dustpan and brush from behind the counter. He reappeared and began sweeping up a few sharp pieces of broken crockery.

'You'll be hungry after all that running around.' Pretzel laughed, winking at them both. 'Muffins are on the house!' he announced loudly. There was a cheer from the packed dining room and the usual friendly buzz of the café returned.

'I *am* rather peckish,' Lester mumbled as a waft of freshly baked muffins drifted from the kitchen. 'So-rry, Cookie.'

Perrie tilted her head and frowned. 'A little louder I think,' she said. 'I'm not sure Cookie heard that.' Lester and Cookie's feud had gone on far too long. A meaningful apology, and forgiveness, were the only way forward. Perrie knew this only too well. Her own sister, Pippa, had played pranks on her for years. Once, she had even tinkered with Perrie's potions, causing Perrie to turn into a slimy frog for three whole days. It was an awful experience and it took Perrie time to forgive Pippa.

Lester took a deep breath. 'I *am* sorry Cookie,' he said.

Cookie's face softened, but before she could reply there was a high-pitched shriek from the kitchen and Pretzel came charging back into the seating area.

'Nobody move!' he cried. 'Do *NOT* eat the Berry-licious muffins!' Arms and legs pumping, he frantically set about snatching muffins from bemused customer's plates, hands and mouths and throwing them into his apron pockets. 'Nothing to worry about,' he said loudly for all to hear, 'they're just not quite cooked. I'll just pop them back in the oven!'

With an apron full of muffins, he returned to where the girls and their friends were standing and beckoned them closer. 'Oh, my goodness,' he hissed, 'this is a catastrophe! Listen!' He held one muffin up and they all leaned in to listen.

It was making a very strange sound indeed. It was snoring! The muffin was actually snoring!

'Is that what I think it is?' gasped Noelle. She could hardly believe her ears.

Chapter 19

Gizmo streaks away

Pretzel was downhearted.

'Cookie, I'm terribly sorry,' he wailed. 'I must have picked the wrong berries from the Wellness Woods. You know me, I was probably so busy singing that I just didn't hear the noise of the snoreberries and I've managed to mix them up in the basket.'

Lester put his ear to Pretzel's apron where the muffins were gathered. It sounded like afternoon nap time at the elf nursery in there. *I wouldn't mind a nap,* he thought.

'Now, Pretzel, let's not panic,' Cookie said. 'These berries only make you sleepy for a few hours and we've only made one batch of these muffins today.'

Eve and Noelle looked at each other. They weren't sure they liked the sound of this.

'Now, due to your quick thinking, we have gathered up all the remaining muffins,' continued Cookie. 'Miss

Jolly took the rest, didn't she?'

Pretzel was thoughtful. 'Yes. Yes, she did... for the Elfland Adventure Park! Oh, my goodness! This is terrible!'

The Elfland Adventure Park was the place to go for a fun day out and some elf relaxation. There were all sorts of exciting activity tents, arts and crafts lessons and well-being classes. As lovely as a dream-filled sleep could be, that wasn't quite what you would be expecting on a day trip to Elfland Adventures. Any elf eating one of the snoreberry muffins would not get what they bargained for. They would miss all the fun and spend the whole-time snoozing.

Eve leaned on the counter and rolled out the map that Mr Arwin had given them. Noelle ran her finger across the page and pointed to Elfland Adventures. It sounded like a great place and, quite apart from the mission at hand, both the girls were keen to see the attraction for themselves.

'And Eleuia, what did he eat?' Eve asked, wondering if he was simply sleeping peacefully somewhere.

'Eleuia sat at that corner table and enjoyed his usual order,' explained Cookie, pointing towards a smaller table beneath one of the windows. 'He had a Springle Star Delight snow cone and a cup of tea, waved goodbye and left. I heard him tell one of the other customers that he was off to Stinky Swamp for some reason.'

'Right,' said Eve decisively, 'that's where we need to go next.'

Noelle moved her finger across the map and located Stinky Swamp. It sounded a lot less inviting than Elfland Adventures, but they had to stay on Eleuia's trail while it was still warm. The clock was ticking loudly against them, and they knew they had to find him soon.

'Let me grab you a Sweet Treat hamper for the journey,' said Pretzel, hurrying back into the kitchen.

Lester rubbed his paws together and licked his chops. This was more like it! Perrie fluttered restlessly around the girls as they plotted a route to Stinky Swamp. The pixie was keen to get going. Pretzel returned with a bulging, tightly buckled wicker hamper, and handed it to Noelle. 'Hopefully, you'll be able to find some clues at the swamp as to Eleuia's whereabouts,' Pretzel said.

'You must go,' said Cookie, 'and so must we! Someone needs to get to Miss Jolly and warn her about those snoreberry muffins before she starts handing them out.'

She turned to address the room.

'Everyone out!' she called. 'Takeaway only. We are closing for the day!'

There was a moment's silence while the Sweet Treats Café customers looked at each other in confusion. Then Pretzel began rounding up the protesting elves, hurriedly ushering them from their wooden stools to the exit at the top of the stairs.

Outside the window, the magenta of Gizmo's scales receded, and he returned to his usual woodland green. The dragon withdrew his eye from the window and clawed stealthily back to the top of the café's toadstool roof. He'd very much enjoyed the chaos caused by Lester, but it was time to get back to business. He had heard everything and wasn't going to let Eve and Noelle get to Eleuia before him. He beat his wings hard and lifted off, spiralling smoothly into the sky, sunlight glinting off his scales. Soon the Sweet Treats Café was a speck below him and the departing customers, just tiny ants. He circled once and streaked away to the north.

Chapter 20

The Stinky Swamp

Hurrying away from the Sweet Treats Café – and unaware of Gizmo's presence above – the adventurers set off, following the route that Noelle had plotted for them. It wasn't long before they were exiting the canopy of trees and entering a clearing quite unlike the others they had come across. Apart from anything else, it was extremely smelly.

Luckily, clouds had bubbled up to weaken the sunlight. Lester was grateful, because he knew that Stinky Swamp could be a whole lot stinkier in the sunshine.

Eve and Noelle screwed up their noses in a vain attempt to block out the powerful stench of dirty socks and mouldy cheese. Much to their disappointment, this place was the opposite of the other places they had visited in Elfland. There seemed little in the way of sweet treats, wonder or excitement to be had here. Just a brown, slimy swamp. Occasional bubbles of pungent gas were breaking the surface and thick blobs of mud flopped back into the lake of gunge.

On the far side, craggy rocks loomed and the whole swamp seemed enclosed by a rickety wooden fence displaying a red warning sign: KEEP OUT. Noelle thought the sign was unnecessary. She couldn't imagine anyone wanting to go in there.

Eve raised her eyebrows. 'Remind me. Why does Eleuia come here?' she asked, peering around the clearing, and trying very hard not to breathe through her nose.

'Though highly unpleasant on the eye *and* the nose, the Stinky Swamp has an essential magic ingredient,' Perrie said. The girls stared hard at the bubbling swamp, struggling to see anything remotely magical about it. Noelle buried her nose in the crook of her arm. It really was the most awful smell. She longed to get away from the swamp and get stuck into the hamper of sweet-smelling goodies that Pretzel had given them.

'When a small sample of this swamp is added to the Dream Stream,' Perrie went on, 'the waters light up and glow so warmly. It is quite the most spectacular sight. The magic created helps to ensure that all the children's wishes flow safely onwards to their destination. It's remarkable that such beauty can come from something so... well... ugly. I suppose it's a lesson that you can find beauty and good in everything if you look hard enough.'

'No need to look that hard where I'm concerned,' said Lester. 'I am, quite obviously, a most beautiful rat both inside and out!' He sucked in his tummy, puffed out his chest and the straining thread on one button of his waistcoat finally gave way. There was a faint twang, and the shiny brass button flew high in the air. It landed with a plop and slipped out of view beneath the muddy surface.

'Hmm. There's always an exception to the rule,' joked Perrie, raising an eyebrow at the embarrassed rodent.

Hiding their laughter, Eve and Noelle turned their backs and moved away to begin searching for any sign of Eleuia and his list. Buddy trotted along behind with his nose in the air. For once, he didn't seem quite so keen to sniff at everything.

A few metres away, Eve stopped and pointed. In the distance, edging towards them, was a small dark figure. *Finally!* thought Eve. *Perhaps this mysterious person is Eleuia and we can say it's mission accomplished?*

Chapter 21

The Wish Wand comes alive

Perrie fluttered away down the path to get a better look at the stranger heading towards them.

'It's just Bow,' she called as she flew back. 'We met him in the Wellness Woods remember. He's an apprentice at the Leaf Factory.'

Buddy barked and galloped towards Bow, who was approaching slowly under the grey clouds gathering above. As Bow drew nearer, they could see his shoulders were slumped. He was trudging along, holding an oversized magnifying glass which he was using to inspect the ground in front of him. As he entered the clearing, they could see that his pointed ears were drooping through the floppy golden hair that flowed out from under his hat.

Finally, he looked up at the others. He had on his black, thick-rimmed glasses and, underneath them, his eyes were wide and brimming with tears.

Perrie immediately fluttered to his side. 'Bow, how awful to see you looking so sad!' she exclaimed. She knew he was concerned about Eleuia and what had become of him. "Try not to worry Bow. We'll find him." Bow chewed on his bottom lip and stared at the floor, unable to speak for a moment. It looked like Perrie's kind words might cause him to burst into tears. He didn't want his voice to crack in front of everyone. Eleuia was his hero – his role model. What could possibly have happened to him?

'It's very nice to see you again, Bow,' said Eve softly, sliding the Wish Wand from her belt. She stepped forward and bent down to try and see the expression on his face. She caught sight of one fat tear as it fell from his eye. It rolled slowly down one lens of his glasses and plopped onto the path. She knew she had to do something. Maybe it was time to test the powers of the wand that Mr Arwin had given her. 'You seem so sad, Bow. If it's OK, can I use my Wish Wand to grant you some courage and hope?' The wooden wand handle felt warm in her palm. Bow nodded miserably and remained still; face turned down towards the ground. He knew of the power of Wish Wands, but he had never been on the receiving end of a spell.

Eve followed Mr Arwin's earlier instructions and

recited the rhyme:

Wish wand come alive,
Grant these wishes as I count from five,
Hope and courage, happiness too,
Wish wand I believe in you!
Five, four, three, two, one...

She placed a comforting hand on Bow's shoulder, while circling the wand above his head. There were no flashes or bangs, no smoke, or stars, but the effect on Bow was instant. He looked up and smiled for the first time that day. His back straightened, his shoulders stretched back confidently, and he took a deep breath.

'Thank you, kind Eve. I couldn't speak for fear of

crying. I've been looking everywhere for Eleuia. I knew he would need to come here to collect a sample from the swamp. I've been looking for clues to his whereabouts, but I've had no success.' Bow held up the magnifying glass as evidence of his efforts. Lester's sharp-toothed face loomed large and terrifying in the lens and he quickly lowered it to his side.

'Sometimes you just need to take a moment to breathe and think,' said Perrie. 'My mind can go all jumbly when it's racing with worries. I just stand still for a while and take deep breaths. It really helps.'

Eve, Noelle and Lester thought that taking a deep breath might not be the best idea while they were standing next to the Stinky Swamp, but Bow seemed unbothered by the stench, and he took a few big gulps of air.

Lester was keen to get going and leave this terrible pong behind. 'So, we have established that Eleuia is not here. Can we go now?' he asked impatiently.

'Yes. You must go,' said Bow, looking at the sky. 'We don't have much time and Eleuia is definitely not here. The last person to see him was Miss Jolly, I think. I bumped into her on the woodland path back there.'

'Miss Jolly?' Eve and Noelle cried. The girls crowded round Bow, and Perrie fluttered nearer. 'Did she have a basket of Sweet Treat Café muffins with her?' she asked urgently.

Bow was perplexed by Perrie's question. 'Yes. Yes,

she did actually. She said that Eleuia took two for his journey. She offered me one, but I said no thank you. I don't much like the berry ones.'

Chapter 22

Bow finds a clue

It seemed likely that Eleuia had mistakenly eaten not one, but *two* of the snoreberry muffins. Eve, Noelle, Bow and Perrie huddled up and all started talking at once. This was new and worrying information. Nobody was sure of the effects of *two* muffins.

'All this kerfuffle and Eleuia is probably fast asleep on a comfy pillow of moss somewhere.' Lester sighed. It was way past time for his afternoon nap, and he was quite envious at the thought of Eleuia enjoying a nice little snooze.

Buddy had padded away from the chattering children and was circling a patch of grass, nose close to the ground. He began to whimper and whine, and everyone turned to see what might be bothering him. 'What's that crazy dog up to now?' asked Eve, hands on hips.

Bow trotted over to the circling canine and peered at the ground through the lens of his magnifying glass.

'Aha!' he cried, plucking something from the grass and holding it aloft between thumb and forefinger.

'What is it?' asked Noelle, squinting. She couldn't see anything. Bow held out his palm so they could all get a better look.

'Muffin crumbs!' he said, triumphantly. 'Well done, clever dog!' Bow turned back to the grass, magnifier to one eye, and began pacing away from them, seemingly following a trail.

'It looks very much as if Eleuia began eating the muffins here and set off in this direction,' he said thoughtfully. 'He must have collected the sample from the swamp and set off for the Leaf Factory. All we need to do is follow this trail.'

Bow continued towards the edge of the clearing, and, with a shrug, the others fell into step behind him. Eve and Noelle sensed they were finally getting warmer in this bizarre game of hide and seek.

However, in the clearing behind them, Buddy had not yet moved. Normally so keen to scout ahead of the others, he was stock still. Something, or some*one,* had caught his attention. He gave a low growl, barked once, and streaked away in the opposite direction.

Eve whipped around. 'You guys carry on. I'll catch you up.' She stumbled over the uneven ground and set off after Buddy.

Already, her beloved dog was almost out of sight.

Chapter 23

Buddy disappears

Eve had to pick up her pace. She called to Buddy but apparently, he was no longer listening to his owner. He galloped around the winding bank of the swamp, leaping over fallen tree trunks and bustling through tall reeds. He was almost at the large and looming rocks on the far side. Eve tripped and stumbled in her effort to keep up.

'Buddy, come back!' she called desperately as her dog finally disappeared from view. She had to slow down to catch her breath and she glanced back at the others. They hadn't gone too far. It was painstaking work, following a trail of muffin crumbs.

She stopped and listened.

'Buddy where are you?' she shouted. Distant barking echoed in reply. As she drew nearer to the dark, forbidding rocks, she spied a fracture in the stone – a jagged gap that she thought she could just about squeeze through if she turned sideways. She did so and, as she shuffled through, the rough surface of the rock scuffed painfully at one of her cheeks and clawed at her clothes.

A few awkward side steps further, just as she was beginning to panic in the confined space, she was through. She staggered back into the light and found herself in another small area of swamp, previously hidden from view. This would have been a strange discovery in itself, but it was what Eve found in the centre of the festering pool that froze her in her tracks.

Buddy was barking furiously and leaping around on the muddy shore. In the centre was a creature that Eve had only read about in books. She could hardly believe her eyes. There, thrashing in the bubbling, stinking slime, was... a dragon!

Nervously, Eve fumbled for Buddy's collar and shrank back towards the gap in the rocks. They crouched there, staring. Thick mud had coated much of the creature's body and tail, but Eve could see fabulous pearlescent green scales glinting. Along its spine were vicious-looking spikes that appeared to be fading from scarlet to grey before their very eyes.

The dragon looked to be in quite a panic and perhaps that colour change was an indication that it was tiring.

Its great wings were heavy with oozy mud and, try as it might, the dragon didn't look like it was going to break free. Its great mouth was filled with razor-sharp teeth, but its eyes were wide and wild with fear. In one claw, the dragon appeared to be clutching a scroll of some sort, though this too was heavy with sludge, and it slopped and slapped as the dragon writhed.

Gizmo's terrified eyes swivelled, and he looked at Eve. He had finally been discovered but this meddling little girl didn't know everything. Gizmo had not yet found Eleuia but he *had* found the Star Wish list.

Despite his predicament, he wasn't about to let that list go and he gripped the sodden scroll even tighter. In fact, it was the act of retrieving the list that had got him stuck in the swamp in the first place. Spotting it from on high, he had dived eagerly for it without paying attention to where he was going to land. It was a foolish, and possibly fatal, mistake.

Eve stepped forward, out of the shadow of the rock and back onto the shore of the pool. She could see that the creature was in terrible difficulty and, though she was scared, she knew she had to be kind and help. There was no time to fetch the others. She had to act. Now.

Reaching to her waist, she again withdrew the Wish Wand from her belt and held it out towards where the dragon was flailing and starting to sink beneath the surface. She noticed a tremor in her hand as magical words flooded into her mind.

Wish Wand I believe in you,
This beautiful dragon believes in you too,
Help to calm his troubled mind,
I know, deep down, he's good and kind,
Grant him strength and pain no more,
Help him leave this swamp and soar.

A wave of calm washed over Gizmo. Having recited the words of the spell, Eve was now standing and watching him with a warm, encouraging smile. Nobody had looked at Gizmo with such kindness and care in a very long time. The emotion he felt was confusing but there was no time to dwell. His wings suddenly broke free from their sludgy bonds and he reared up, beating them hard. With a great sucking and squelching sound, and a powerful flick of his tail, the dragon lifted his body up and out of the thick, cloying mud. As he did so, a wave of scarlet rippled through his spines. He circled the cove, just metres above Eve's head. Buddy leapt and barked, and Eve had to hang on to her elf hat as a blast of air from Gizmo's great wings threatened to send it flying from her head and tumbling into the swamp.

Eve thought she caught a glimpse of something in the dragon's eyes. Was it understanding? Gratitude? She wasn't sure. She wanted the creature to stay, to find out more about it.

But as she waved and beckoned to it, the dragon wheeled away from her and spiralled into the sky. It was soon a tiny silhouette against the clouds above.

Chapter 24

Never meddle with dark spells

Lester was *not* happy.

'I have done everything asked of me on this mission so far,' he screeched, 'but I am *not* going in there!'

The trail of muffin crumbs had led the girls and their Elfland guides south to the edge of an area known as the Enchanted Forest. After Eve had raced to tell the others about her incredible encounter with the dragon, the search party had moved off once more, nervously listening out for the slow beat of a dragon's wings and following the trail of tiny clues that they desperately hoped would lead them to Eleuia. Time was fast running out.

The Enchanted Forest was the most beautiful area of Elfland, home to diverse and fabulous wildlife and where the trees were heavy with succulent fruits and berries. Once, long ago, it had been a popular destination for all the inhabitants of Elfland but only a brave few ventured in there now. One of those was Pretzel, who occasionally tiptoed in with a small basket to collect a few delicious ingredients for the Sweet Treats Café. He never lingered too long and never went too far. It was just too dangerous.

And Lester knew it!

Perrie, keen to explain Lester's outburst, looked up from the trail of crumbs that stretched ahead of them and turned to Eve and Noelle. 'This is the Enchanted Forest,' she said solemnly. 'Home to Coletta.' There was a sudden note of fear in Perrie's voice and the girls exchanged worried looks. This wasn't at all like the happy, courageous pixie they had come to know. They found it hard to believe that anywhere in Elfland could be a place of fear. It seemed so full of kindness and joy.

'Who or *what* is Coletta?' Eve asked.

'Let's rest for a moment and I'll explain,' said Perrie, landing on a small toadstool next to the path. Eve and Noelle knelt down in front of her on the grass whilst Buddy stretched out in a pool of sunshine. They looked expectantly at the pixie. Bow and Lester stood some way off, nervously shuffling their feet and talking in hushed tones. They knew the story of Coletta. Everyone in Elfland did.

'Three years ago, Coletta was one of Santa's favourite elves. She was kind, funny and popular and she could build and wrap the most wonderful presents faster than any other elf in the land. She flourished and thrived in the warm glow of Santa's attention and praise. Life for

Coletta was perfect.' Perrie paused to make sure she had the girls' full attention.

'But that all ended one fateful day when a group of new elf recruits arrived in the workshop. One elf, named Jingle, caught everyone's eye. He was young and energetic and simply bursting with ideas for new gifts and new wrapping styles. He immediately set about creating fresh new colour combinations, and styles of bows to give presents an extra shine.' Perrie smiled, thinking about Jingle. She hoped Eve and Noelle would have the opportunity to meet him. 'He brought joy to the workshop, to Santa, and all the other elves. All except one.'

'Let me guess. Coletta?' Eve said, shuffling forward. Eve and Noelle were hanging on Perrie's every word.

'Yes, poor Coletta quickly grew jealous of Jingle. Even though she was still loved and respected, just as she always had been, she could not bear to see another elf succeed and overshadow her work. The more fabulous Jingle's ideas, the more bitter Coletta became. She festered in her bitterness, until her jealousy grew so strong that she broke the simple rule:

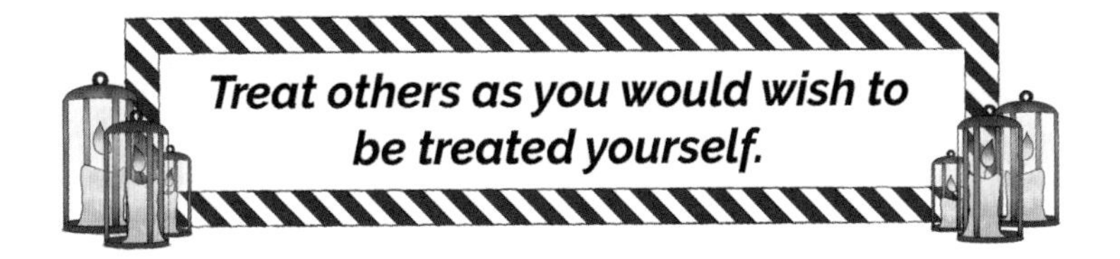

'Oh dear,' said Eve. She knew how important it was to be kind to others.

'In secret, she searched the land for a rare spell to turn Jingle into a goblin and have him cast out from the workshop. Coletta gathered the spell ingredients and plotted to destroy Jingle. She was so consumed by anger and upset that she completely forgot that often, our feelings and actions are like a mirror,' Perrie said sadly.

'Well, what happened?' cried Noelle, eager to hear the end of the story. Lester and Bow had returned to the group, and here Lester picked up the tale.

'Coletta worked on her potion for many weeks, but you should never meddle with dark spells,' he said gravely. 'Only Mr Arwin has the power to control those. It seems that Coletta's spell backfired, and she only succeeded in turning *herself* into a goblin. So, angry, and ashamed, she escaped here to the Enchanted Forest.'

'And here *we* are,' said Perrie, gesturing at the trees ahead of them. 'She has hidden here, in the Enchanted Forest, ever since.' Perrie sighed. 'What was once the most beautiful forest in Elfland has become a place of unkindness and fear. A few people have been brave enough to enter, but an encounter with Coletta is never a nice experience. She plays the most awful pranks on anyone and everyone she finds.'

'Well, *she* sounds delightful,' said Noelle with a nervous gulp.

'That's not the worst of it!' cried Lester, ignoring Perrie's warning look. 'No one is sure if Coletta has any of the potion left or if she could cast her spell again. I've no desire to be turned into a Lester-sized goblin. I'd rather stay my handsome self, thank you very much! And *THAT* is why I am *NOT* going in there! Even Remi, the Sleepy Elf, doesn't dare to venture near Coletta. Once, Remi tried to help Coletta, explaining that calming her mind and enjoying a peaceful night's sleep may have been just the remedy she needed. Coletta chased Remi right out of the Enchanted Forest!' Lester said, twitching his whiskers.

'Who is Remi?' asked Eve, frowning.

'Remi is Elfland's Sleepy Elf. A Sleepy Elf is the guardian of the Grand Sleep Secret and is in charge of helping children get the best possible rest and relaxation. Remi is telepathic and can even teleport too!' said Perrie.

'My favourite elf,' said Lester, shrugging at Bow. 'Sorry.'

'You'll meet Remi at the end of your adventure. They will help you get home,' Perrie advised. 'But for now, we need to focus on Eleuia. Let's hope he has NOT crossed paths with Coletta.'

Lester folded his arms and turned his back with a loud 'harumph'.

'But whyever would Eleuia want to venture in there if it's so dangerous?' asked Eve, getting back to her feet.

She was starting to think they might have been wrong to follow the muffin crumb trail.

'When snoreberries start to work, they make you drowsy and dull your senses before you slip into a deep sleep,' explained Perrie. 'The path through the Enchanted Forest *is* the quickest route to the Leaf Factory but normally Eleuia would skirt around it. I fear, in his sleepy state, he may have stumbled straight on and into terrible danger.'

'Gosh!' cried Eve anxiously. 'We need to find him before Coletta does!'

Chapter 25

Journey into the Enchanted Forest

It took some time for them to convince Lester to summon his courage and follow them into the Enchanted Forest. Eve almost had to use the Wish Wand. He remained extremely nervous, and all of his senses were on high alert as they crept along the path. Every sound from the undergrowth set his heart thudding loudly in his chest and he soon decided it would be better to stay close to the others rather than scuff sulkily along behind.

Anxious as they were, Eve and Noelle couldn't help but be amazed by this part of Elfland. The forest floor was carpeted with strange plants and exotic blooms and the majestic trees were alive with birds of every imaginable colour. They flapped and glided between the branches, and, with a thousand different tweets and calls, they sang to the intruders below. Were they communicating a welcome or a warning? It was hard to know, but to Eve and Noelle the music was just wonderful and so comforting.

At ground level, insects were buzzing lazily amongst bushes laden with berries and fruits and occasionally the adventurers' disturbed clouds of colourful butterflies as they pushed through the long grasses. They erupted into the air and fluttered around them as they made their way cautiously forwards.

'Eleuia, where are you?' Lester muttered under his breath. He wasn't soothed one bit by the sights and sounds of the Enchanted Forest. He knew the danger that lay within.

'It's such a beautiful place,' whispered Eve. 'How could anything unpleasant happen here?' She was mesmerised.

Suddenly, everything changed.

Silence.

The choir of birds stopped singing and, in a flurry of flapping wings and rustling leaves, they were gone, fleeing into the sky above. The buzz of insects ceased and the butterflies that had just moments before been dancing merrily around their heads scattered, weaving away through the tree trunks. On the forest floor, panicked creatures scampered for burrows and the comparative safety of shadowy nooks.

'Coletta,' hissed Perrie ominously.

The sudden silence was deafening.

Eve, Noelle, Lester, and Bow huddled together.

Eve pulled Buddy close, and they crouched as glowering dark clouds drifted across the sun and the forest grew instantly colder and darker. Perrie buzzed and fizzed around them, searching for any sign of the goblin.

In Eve's arms, Buddy barked and wriggled. She tried to calm him, but he kicked his legs, and she lost her grip. He wrestled free and galloped further into the trees.

'Buddy, no!' cried Eve, running after him. Quick as a flash, the others jumped up and hurried along behind, hot on her heels.

Buddy had not gone far. They found him whimpering

and fussing around a patch of toadstools just a short distance away. Lester was terrified and wished the human's dog would just be quiet. This day was going from bad, to worse, to absolutely terrible. He felt certain that Buddy must have announced their arrival to Coletta.

Concerned, Eve knelt before Buddy and held his face in her hands. He seemed to be barring her way. He refused to let her take another step.

'What's wrong with him?' whispered Noelle, leaning over Eve's shoulder.

Perrie zoomed up and into a hover above them. Perhaps she could catch sight of Coletta before it was too late. She twisted and turned in mid-air, peering into the shadows.

Meanwhile, Bow – equally bemused by the dog's behaviour – had begun examining the grass around them. He held his magnifying glass to his eye and inspected the ground just beyond where Buddy had halted Eve in her tracks.

Suddenly, forgetting the danger they were in, Bow gave a triumphant shout. 'Goodness! What a clever dog you have!' Bow was staring in delighted disbelief at something tucked in the blades of grass at his feet.

'Shhhhhhhh!' hissed Lester, waving his paws. 'Stop shouting!'

'Eleuia! We found Eleuia!' Bow cried, joyfully passing the magnifying glass for Eve to see.

She grabbed it from his outstretched hand and held it to her own eye.

She was nonplussed. 'Where?' she asked. 'I don't see anything!'

Bow pointed and, finally, she saw him.

Chapter 26

Coletta's nasty surprise

Eleuia was sitting on the back of a friendly ladybird that had come to rest on a blade of grass. He was wearing an outfit similar in style to Eve and Noelle's and all the other elves they had met except his tunic was the same blue colour as Mr Arwins. But Eve could tell he was important. A shock of auburn hair flowed from under his grand elf hat and his tunic seemed more elaborately embroidered than their own. He was staring at her with bright blue eyes and his arms were waving frantically. Through the magnifying glass, he looked like he was shouting something, but he was so small that Eve could not hear a word of whatever it was he was trying to say. He looked worried though.

She quickly alerted Perrie and the excited pixie swooped down to help. Perrie was overjoyed to have found her friend but dismayed at his miniature condition. She thanked the ladybird and scooped the Wellness Elf into her arms.

'Oh, Eleuia, what has Coletta done to you?' she murmured sadly. He would never have got out of the Enchanted Forest on his own. Now perhaps they could make their escape and work out how to return Eleuia to his proper size so that he could complete his vital task.

Lester was relieved that Eleuia had been found but he knew they weren't out of danger yet and he was on full alert. While the others continued their hushed conversation and muted celebrations, Lester kept his eyes peeled for trouble.

He was the first to spot her. As he stared at a gnarled tree across the clearing, there was sudden movement in the trunk. Lester gave a tiny, terrified squeak, unable to find the words to warn his friends. The rough bark of the tree shifted again, and one evil-looking eye opened as a bodily form stepped forwards and away from the trunk. Coletta had been there all along, camouflaged to avoid detection. She grinned at Lester, revealing sharp, yellow-stained fangs. Her rust-red hair looked greasy, and it drooped to the shoulders of a torn and grubby purple dress.

'Hello, *friends*,' snarled Coletta, taunting them with a cloth pouch that she raised towards them.

Lester gulped. He knew that the contents of that pouch were bound to have devastating consequences if any of it should fall upon them.

Finally, Lester found his voice and stammered a warning to the others.

'C-C-C-C-COLETTA!' he shouted, clawing at the hem of Noelle's skirt, and pointing a trembling finger at the goblin.

Eve, Noelle, and Bow whirled around in alarm. Buddy sat back on his haunches, lowered his head, and gave a fierce growl from deep inside his chest. Instinctively, Eve reached for the Wish Wand in her belt. There must be a spell that would come to her, to help the goblin and save them all. But Perrie fluttered quickly to her shoulder.

'Kind Eve, many a wise elf has tried, but the power of change can only come from within,' she whispered quickly. 'No magic spells will help Coletta and nor will your Wish Wand.' Staring at the wicked goblin's glittering black eyes, Perrie knew Coletta's heart was still dark with jealousy and anger. She would not allow light to shine in.

Not today anyway.

It was eerily silent as they stared at each other. Lester scurried back behind Bow's ankle, trembling with fear. It wasn't Coletta's appearance that made him shake, for Lester knew that real beauty lay within. Coletta's curse had expressed on the *outside*, who she had become on the *inside*. A few wise elves had visited the forest to try and help her before. They had pleaded with her to set aside her jealousy and bitterness towards others, especially Jingle, but it had all been in vain. Coletta had rejected their advice and ignored their guidance. She didn't believe that she, and she alone, held the key to breaking the curse she had accidentally placed upon herself. With every resentful act of nastiness, she grew ever uglier.

As she leered at them across the clearing, a fresh new wart grew on her cheek. It was a warning that something very unpleasant was about to happen to the Enchanted Forest visitors.

There was only one thing for it.

'Run!' cried Perrie desperately as Coletta suddenly lunged forward and began fumbling with the strings that held the pouch closed. 'Quickly, get out of the forest as fast as you can!'

Chapter 27

Gizmo saves the day

Lester did not need to be told twice and he was already scurrying back the way they had come as fast as his paws would carry him. In a flash, Bow had caught up with him and he snatched at the back of Lester's waistcoat as he sprinted past. Little legs still pumping, Lester was lifted into the air.

'Hang on, Lester!' Bow bellowed as they accelerated to outrun the goblin.

Dazed by recent events, Eve and Noelle were momentarily frozen to the spot but Perrie, who had just zipped past with Eleuia clinging on for dear life, U-turned and implored them to hurry. The girls snapped awake and charged after the buzzing pixie with Buddy in hot pursuit.

They ran like the wind, leaping over toadstools and fallen branches, fleeing through long grasses, and leaving a trail of beheaded flowers and fluttering petals in their wake. When they came to the curtains of ivy and vines that hung from branches, they swept them aside with their hands and crashed onward. Eve dared not pause to look over her shoulder, but she felt sure she could hear the galloping of goblin feet close behind. They ran. And ran. And ran.

Finally, just as they felt their lungs might burst, Perrie turned to peer back. 'Wait!' she gasped. 'I think Coletta may have given up the chase.'

Behind them, they could see no sign of the goblin and, as they staggered to a halt, the forest fell silent once more, except for their loud panting. Lester slithered from Bow's grasp and slumped to the forest floor. He was feeling queasy after all that jolting and jiggling. He was wondering if it might, perhaps, be safer to continue the journey under his own steam. Eve and Noelle were bent double, hands-on knees, trying to catch their breath. Buddy circled them, tongue lolling.

Perrie looked again at her friend. 'Oh Eleuia,' she said, 'don't you worry, we'll get some Growth Glitter when we reach the Leaf Factory and get you back to your rightful size.' She turned to the others. 'We must—'

Whatever Perrie was going to say, she did not get a chance to finish her sentence. For there, suddenly emerging from the trees nearby, was Coletta.

Buddy whined and the terrified search party huddled together once more as Coletta edged closer to them, grinning triumphantly. The pouch was open in her hand and a thin trickle of twinkling grey dust cascaded from it.

'You thought you could outrun *me*? In *my* forest?' She cackled. 'You never stood a chance. And now, I'm going to shrink you and turn you *all* into goblins. You'll be my obedient, snivelling little servants. Star Wishes will be no more. Elfland will descend into despair and then *nobody* will be better than me.'

All hope seemed to be gone. Bow's shoulders slumped once more and Lester clung to his leg, quivering with fear. Perrie's wings drooped. She was all out of ideas as Coletta took another, menacing step towards them.

'What are we going to do?' wailed Noelle, glancing at Eve.

Coletta raised the hand that was holding the pouch and sneered at them. Just as she was about to celebrate victory and launch the dust at them, Eve summoned all of her courage and her fear melted away. She raised her own hand, in which she held the wand, and closed her eyes. A wave of strength journeyed from her feet to the tip of her elf hat and she spoke loudly and clearly into the forest.

Magnificent forest, hear our plea,
The magic of Elfland, we ask you to see,
Light over darkness is magic too,
Help to make our wishes come true.

Coletta began to laugh. 'What ridiculous nonsense was that?' she cried. 'Nobody will come to your aid, foolish child. As if any of *you* could possibly beat me?' For many long moments, the only sound they could hear echoing around the forest was Coletta's cruel laughter.

Then, suddenly, they all became aware of other sounds. The sounds they had heard when they first entered this beautiful place. And what followed was like nothing that Perrie, Lester, Bow or Eleuia had ever witnessed before.

As though answering Eve's call and no longer fearful of Coletta, the animals of the Enchanted Forest began to return. Mesmerising music filled the air once more as the birds swept back through the branches, singing, and almost knocking Coletta from her feet as the multi-coloured flock flapped and fluttered around her. Simultaneously, great clouds of butterflies and insects exploded from the undergrowth and buzzed haphazardly through the tree trunks to join the battle. The panicked goblin clawed wildly at the air to try and ward them off and the pouch fell from her grasp.

With Coletta distracted, and without her magic dust, it was time to make their escape. Eve jammed the wand back in her belt. Crouching low beneath the circling birds, they looked around them for the best route out.

Before they could decide, a huge black shadow fell across them and a cold blast of wind knocked them all from their feet, including Coletta. Leaves and dust kicked up by the blast of air blinded them for a moment and they had to shield their eyes. Eve and Noelle were forced to hang on to their hats.

Drowning out the forest sounds, there came the woomph, woomph, woomph of great, beating wings and the thud of heavy feet. The ground shook.

'Climb aboard!' urged Gizmo. The dragon folded his wings, unfurled his tail, and looked at Eve. They did not need a second invitation and, led by Eve, the adventurers clambered awkwardly onto Gizmo's back, hauling each other up the dragon's slippery scales.

'NOOOOOOOO!' cried Coletta, defeated. She furiously snatched up the pouch and hurled it at Gizmo as he lifted into the air with his passengers clinging tightly to his back. Caught by the draft of his wings, most of the grey, twinkling dust scattered harmlessly away but one small speck settled on Lester's tail.

Worst day ever! Lester thought. He stared in horror as his tail began to shrink.

Chapter 28

The flight to the factory

Their stomachs lurched wildly as Gizmo ascended. The powerful beat of his wings lifted them easily through the tree canopy and away from immediate danger.

Buddy was sitting up front proudly. He had already taken up position between Gizmo's shoulder blades like some sort of bizarre dragon-driver. The wind swept up his ears and set them flapping behind him. Eve and Noelle, slightly more nervous about their first flight on a dragon, clung to Gizmo's scales and squinted against the on-rushing air. Just behind them, Bow took one glance at the fast-disappearing ground and screwed his eyes tight shut. He had discovered that he wasn't a fan of heights at all.

Feeling very despondent *and* tiny, Lester clambered into the relative safety of one of Bow's pockets where he curled up in a ball and cursed Coletta's Diminishing Dust.

This really was turning out to be a *very* bad day indeed. Perrie and Eleuia found a sheltered spot behind one of the great spikes that ran down Gizmo's spine. Though fast, there was no way Perrie could have kept up with the dragon. She folded her wings and they both hunkered down. As they rose into the sky, Coletta's cries of rage rapidly receded beneath them, and the last few notes of the birds' beautiful singing drifted away on the breeze.

They soared gracefully.

Gizmo's heart was soaring too. It was a sensation that was unfamiliar to him... and he liked it. Very much. He'd instinctively known he *had* to repay the kindness that Eve had shown him back at the swamp and, in doing so, he felt very good indeed. Without realising it, and perhaps for the first time, he had followed that golden Elfland rule:

His rescue mission was honourable, a far cry from his intentions when he first heard that Eleuia had disappeared. He flew on, swooping joyfully through clouds and exploding into bright sunshine.

Eve and Noelle held on to their hats and peered over the edge of Gizmo's wide back. Below, they could see all of Elfland's beauty laid out before them. They could see many of the places they had already been and others they had yet to discover.

'Where do we go next?' shouted Noelle over the noise of the rushing wind. 'We've found Eleuia. What now?'

Eve looked at her friend and shrugged but Perrie shouted the answer, and her words just reached the girls' ears.

'We need to get to the Leaf Factory,' cried Perrie. 'That would have been Eleuia's next stop and it's where we might find a spell to return him and Lester to their rightful sizes.'

Eve nodded and turned towards the dragon's great head.

'Dragon!' she shouted. He seemed to cock his head and half turn to listen. 'We need to get to the Leaf Factory. Do you know where that is? Can you take us there?'

With an almost imperceptible nod, Gizmo suddenly banked left and went into a steep dive.

Everyone screamed in alarm.

Chapter 29

A noisy welcome

Gizmo's passengers had to cling even more tightly, their knuckles white as they gripped the edges of his scales. Inside Bow's pocket, the dragon's sudden, terrifying move caused Lester to tumble over into a dusty, crumb-filled corner.

As Gizmo pulled out of his death-defying dive and Eve and Noelle could breathe once more, the air grew cooler. A crisp wintry breeze and the familiar sweet smells of the woods returned. He skimmed smoothly over the treetops then glided down below the woodland canopy into a wide gap between tall tree trunks. They were now skimming the forest floor, Gizmo's wings flicking the leaves and branches as they powered onwards. Eve and Noelle, still holding on to their elf hats, sat up and peered ahead where a wondrous building was coming into view.

The Leaf Factory. A grand and sacred building that played an important role in preparing children's Star Wishes for their final journey. It was like a golden castle, shining in the late afternoon sunshine. Gizmo banked gently to circle the great building and to search for a good landing site. Eve and Noelle counted six turrets with six red flags fluttering from them. As the girls looked down into the courtyard, hundreds of elves were hurrying out of doorways to wave up at them. Eve and Noelle grinned happily at each other and waved back.

Gizmo completed his circle of the factory, adjusted his wing beat and reared up, making ready to land. His passengers braced themselves against his scales, but they needn't have worried. Huge as he was, Gizmo was conscious of the elves in his care, and he surprised them by landing as lightly as a feather just in front of the magnificent building. Dust and leaves that were kicked up by the downdraft quickly settled and he crouched to allow his passengers to disembark.

The group wasted no time. With a satisfied bark, Buddy leapt to the grass and Eve, Noelle and Bow swung their legs over Gizmo's great back and slithered to the ground. Bow stumbled drunkenly and, at last, fully opened his eyes. His legs had turned to jelly, and he was profoundly relieved to find his elf shoes back on terra firma. Perrie unfolded her wings, scooped Eleuia into her arms and fluttered down to join them.

Eve turned to the dragon. 'Thank you,' she said, laying a gentle hand on his great head. She smiled.

Though the dragon was huge, with fearsome-looking teeth that could surely have made a quick meal of his passengers, Gizmo's eyes seemed to twinkle with gentle kindness. His cheeks flushed pink. He was not used to receiving such positive attention, or indeed any attention at all. He turned shyly away and shuffled his monstrous claws.

'Best day ever!' Noelle cried, jumping, and punching the air. An escape from a wicked goblin on the back of a dragon was going to be very hard to top.

Before anyone had time to agree, there was a loud grinding of iron hinges and the Leaf Factory's grand wooden gates began to open. From within there came a great cheer of tiny voices and, through the slowly opening doors, a large group of elves tumbled, grinning, and waving happily. Rushing out, they seemed apprehensive of Gizmo, and they gave him a wide berth, but they were thrilled to see Perrie with Eleuia in her arms. They crowded around the adventurers, all talking loudly at once. Perrie spoke quickly to one of the elves and he scurried back the way he had come, pushing through the on-rushing crowd.

Eve and Noelle were quite overwhelmed by all the excitement and the noise of chatter was deafening. Suddenly, however, there was silence. The crowd of elves parted to allow the oldest looking of the elves to reach them. It appeared that he had great authority here.

'Perhaps he's the factory foreman,' Noelle whispered.

In both hands, and with great care, he was carrying a small vial containing some familiar-looking, glittering dust. *Growth Glitter!* thought Eve. She could hardly wait to meet Eleuia properly. It had been quite an adventure!

Inclining her head, Perrie graciously accepted the vial from the elf elder and gently placed Eleuia on the ground in front of her. There was a murmur of anticipation amongst the crowd, and they shuffled backwards nervously. Perrie fluttered above their heads, weaving, and twisting in the air to encourage the elves to retreat yet further and widen the circle. She needed room to work.

She returned to the centre and spiralled above the spot where Eleuia stood, ant-like, on the ground. She flipped the cork from the top of the vial and glittering dust showered the tiny Wellness Elf. Perrie began to chant.

I scatter upon you, this magic dust,
Wellness Elf! Come back to us!
No longer will you be so small
Stand among us, brave and tall,
Return to your true shape and size,
Grow back at once before our eyes.

The magic was ignited instantly. The ground beneath their feet trembled and golden smoke began to billow from the area where Perrie had placed Eleuia.

Already difficult to spot amongst the blades of grass, the tiny elf disappeared completely in the clouds of yellow vapour. The crowd pushed forward once more, desperate for the magic to undo Coletta's spell.

Failure was unthinkable.

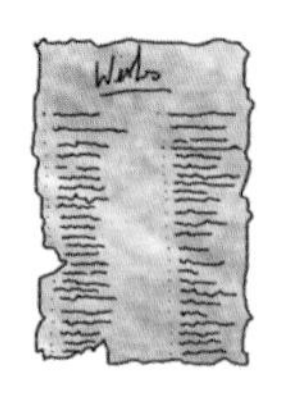

Chapter 30

Eleuia takes charge

Eleuia's wiry hair was auburn and unruly. It poked out in all directions from under his hat. A spray of freckles decorated his cheeks and button nose, and his eyes twinkled with mischief. He turned slowly, grinning broadly at the crowd. The magic had done its job and Eleuia was back to his rightful size.

As the last tendrils of smoke drifted away, Eve and Noelle could finally get a good view of the elf they had been searching for. There was certainly an air of importance about him, and they gawked at the beautiful embroidery on his Wellness Elf uniform. The crowd pressed forward and cheered loudly. The elves were mightily relieved to have Eleuia returned to them safe and sound.

Eleuia raised his hands to quieten the crowd of chattering elves. 'Greetings, old friends!' he said, raising his voice so all could hear. 'And new!' He smiled welcomingly at Eve and Noelle. 'Thank you to all who played a part in my rescue.'

Lester, still a fraction of his former size, clawed at the inside of Bow's pocket and managed to haul his head over the edge to see what was going on.

Eleuia spotted him. 'Lester? Do not worry. I believe Perrie has just enough Growth Glitter left to return you to the handsomely sized chap you used to be.' He winked at Perrie.

Turning back to the crowd, Eleuia addressed the elves once more. This time, his voice was solemn.

'I'm afraid I have some bad news,' he continued. 'I am sorry to report that, in my dazed and sleepy state, I managed to lose the list.' He placed his hands wearily on his hips and his head drooped.

There was a collective intake of breath as the huddle of elves gasped in horror. Hands flew to gaping mouths, heads shook, hat bells jingled and there was a crescendo of panicked, urgent conversation. They were already running behind schedule; they had been ready to work at lightning speed to scribe the children's wishes from the list onto their leaves.

But there *was* no list. Calamity!

On the edge of the crowd, Gizmo backed away and glanced down at the Star Wish list still clutched in his claw. It was tatty and mud-spattered, but the scroll held the wishes of a thousand children. Wishes that Gizmo, not so long ago, had wanted to destroy. But now he was torn. He could escape immediately if he wanted to, while everyone's focus was on the Wellness Elf. He could fly to a remote corner of the woods and destroy the list. Nobody would know and if *his* wish could be ignored, then he saw no reason why anyone else's should be granted.

But now, there was an alternative. One that he had not considered before. At least, not until Eve had shown him such gentle kindness and care and he had returned that friendship with his daring rescue. Doing good – doing the right thing – had given him such pleasure and filled him with such warmth and joy that he felt he wanted more of those special emotions.

Again, Eleuia raised his hands to silence the crowd.

'My... *Our* only hope is that some kind inhabitant of Elfland came upon the list and has kept it safe for me until I could be returned to my normal size. I am so sorry, my friends. I fear I have let you all down.'

'It's Cookie's fault really,' Lester piped up from his perch on Bow's pocket. 'If she hadn't baked those muffins with the snoreberries, we'd never be in this mess.'

Perrie heard this and gave Lester a ferocious look. It was no time to be laying the blame at anyone's door. 'Any more talk like that,' she hissed, 'and I might lose what's left of this Growth Glitter.'

'Orrrrrr maybe accidents happen,' Lester said, somewhat panicked by Perrie's threat and upset with himself for raising the matter.

'Or maybe, just maybe, all of this happened to make someone's wish come true,' Eleuia wondered thoughtfully. Taking one step forward, he made to leave the centre of the crowd and the elves shuffled back and created a path for him. Eleuia strode through them, gesturing to calm and quieten them as he did so.

Silence fell once more, but for the distant bird song and soft rumble of the dragon's breathing. Eleuia came to a halt in front of Gizmo's snout, inches from those razor-like teeth. He could feel the dragon's hot breath on his face, and it ruffled his untidy fringe.

Gizmo felt shame. Another new emotion and one he was not keen on *at all*. He knew the choice he had to make. The Wellness Elf stood before him. Expectant. Smiling. Gizmo raised one mighty set of claws and the elves gasped again. This great dragon was not to be trusted. The air crackled with danger. One swipe of those talons could wipe out the entire crowd and the Leaf Factory could be demolished with a flick of his tail. Nervously, the elves shrank back.

The setting sun glinted from Gizmo's scales and new colours rippled through his body. Eleuia remained very still, smiling kindly at the dragon and seemingly oblivious to the mortal danger. There was a pause, and everyone held their breath. Very slowly, Gizmo opened his clenched claw and the torn and muddy wish list dropped into Eleuia's outstretched hands. A great cry of joy erupted from the crowd of elves.

Chapter 31

Gizmo finds happiness

Gizmo was startled and confused by the sudden eruption of noisy happiness at what he had just done. He retreated a few paces, eyeing the whooping and hollering crowd.

'Bow!' Eleuia called, signalling for him to approach. Bow was thrilled that his hero seemed to know his name. Eleuia handed him the rolled-up wish list scroll. 'Thank you for your bravery and dedication in finding me *and* the list. Get to work on this and I will meet you all at the Dream Stream later.' Bow was lost for words. What an honour Eleuia had bestowed upon him. Unsure what to do, he did a sort of awkward curtsy-bow and almost fell over his own feet. Raising the wish list scroll and waving it aloft, he made for the Leaf Factory gates with the crowd of excited elves hurrying along behind him.

Eve was happy. Eleuia *and* the list had been found. Their mission was surely complete. She and Noelle walked over to where Eleuia still stood in front of the dragon. Buddy leapt alongside them and both girls made a fuss of him. Behind them, Perrie set about returning Lester to his original size. She flipped the stopper from the vial and began showering him with the remaining Growth Glitter.

Eve stepped next to Eleuia and they stood in comfortable silence for a moment. They exchanged a knowing look and then Eleuia began to speak gently to the dragon who was crouched and uncertain of his next move.

'Gizmo, the most magnificent creature in all of our land,' pronounced Eleuia, flinging his arms wide. 'No longer must you live lonely in the shadows. You are part of Elfland and always have been. Your strength is grace. You must embrace who you are and be proud of yourself. You have done wonderful, brave and kind things here today and, despite what you may think, you have many friends throughout these woods.'

Eve gently placed both her hands on the side of Gizmo's enormous head. She stretched her arms as wide as they would go and rested her cheek against the dragon's cool scales.

'You saved us, Gizmo. Thank you for being my friend,' she whispered softly.

Friendship? Gizmo turned the idea over in his mind and his eyes twinkled. *I have... friends!* The wish seemingly denied him so long ago had finally come true.

'You will join us at the Dream Stream tonight, Gizmo,' commanded Eleuia. 'After all, we and the list are only safe because of you. It's only right that you are there to enjoy the celebrations with us.'

Joy and gratitude flooded through Gizmo and his scales rippled with vibrant shades of every colour.

In his delight, he stretched his great wings and lifted off, happily circling them before soaring away into the evening sky. He left his new friends on the ground below, laughing, waving, and pointing.

With the list safely behind the grand golden doors of the Leaf Factory and Eleuia returned to normal size, balance in Elfland had been restored. Though far behind schedule, the wishes would still be ready in time to make their final journey along the Dream Stream just a few hours from now. The skilful Leaf Factory elves would see to that.

Chapter 32

One more job to do

Eve and Noelle, and their Elfland friends, looked to the sky and waved until Gizmo was merely a point of golden light on the horizon. He would undoubtedly be back for the celebrations and the Dream Stream ceremony but, for now, he had left his new friends alone with their thoughts.

'What now?' asked Noelle, turning to Eve.

Eve felt the magical Elf Eyes had brought them here, to this remarkable land, to find Eleuia and restore harmony in Elfland. Now that they had achieved that, she felt sure it must be time to return home. It had been an incredible adventure, but she was beginning to miss her mother and father and her cosy bedroom at home. It could only have been a few hours since she and Noelle had snuggled into their sleeping bags, but it already felt like many days ago. After all the excitement, she felt suddenly weary.

Then something occurred to her. They *did* have some unfinished business.

'Oh goodness,' she cried, slapping one hand to her forehead. 'What about the rest of the muffins? We were concentrating so hard on finding Eleuia here that I completely forgot about them.'

Lester was finally returned to his normal size. Perrie's ears pricked and, leaving the moody rodent slumped on the grass, she fluttered quickly over to where Noelle was unfurling the Elfland map.

'You're right!' said Eleuia as he leaned in. 'Those snoreberry muffins are quite hazardous, as I know only too well. Miss Jolly's basket was overflowing with them when I met her on the path. They must not fall into the wrong hands.'

'Cookie and Pretzel set off after Miss Jolly to warn her, but there's no telling if they got to her in time. But look at the map!' said Eve, tracing one finger across the paper. 'Elfland Adventures is such a long way away from here. We'll never get there in time.'

They scratched their heads.

'I have an idea!' cried Eleuia.

'What is it?' chorused the girls. But Eleuia didn't answer. He wandered away from them, mumbling strange words to no one in particular. His face was up turned towards the sky as he spoke.

The girls looked at each other. 'What's up with him?' asked Noelle. 'He's gone a bit weird.'

'If you think that's weird, just wait and see what happens next,' said Lester as he stomped sulkily towards them, paws thrust deep in his waistcoat pockets. He was hungry and tired, but it didn't look like any of them would be going home anytime soon.

Eleuia continued his strange mumbling. Buddy barked.

They all looked west, in the direction that Eleuia appeared to be facing. The sun was quite low now and the girls had to shield their eyes against it. They squinted. Out of the distant sky, just above the treetops, there came an object, travelling fast.

Chapter 33

The remarkable flying machine

'Is that... Gizmo?' Noelle wondered aloud.

But as the object came ever nearer, they could see it did not have wings. Or a tail for that matter. Occasionally, as it weaved, the sides of the object caught the sun's rays and they glittered and shone briefly.

Satisfied, Eleuia turned and grinned at Perrie. They both knew what was coming. Perplexed, the two girls continued to stare and wonder.

A few seconds later, the approaching object took form and Eve and Noelle wondered no more. Rooted to the spot, they panicked for a moment that they might be run over but Eleuia shouted a warning.

'Stand back!' he called as the strange vehicle came to a sliding, screeching halt right where the five friends and Buddy had just been standing. It hovered just inches above the ground, bobbing and thrumming with energy and magic.

'It's a sleigh!' cried Eve.

Buddy barked again and sniffed cautiously at the glittering silver exhaust pipes that snaked down the sides of the vehicle. Noelle's jelly legs had wobbled, and she'd landed heavily on her bottom, but now she picked herself up from the grass. Her eyes were wide, and she gently touched the scarlet paintwork with her fingertips. It was yet another unbelievable sight on a day that had been full of them, and she had to reassure herself it was real.

The sleigh, for that was indeed what it seemed to be, was magnificent. It gleamed with golden swirls and stars and beautiful curves swept elegantly from front to rear. All that was missing was a team of reindeer. But the sleigh seemed to be travelling under its own magical power.

'Is this what I think it is?' Noelle gasped, reaching for Eve's hand, and giving it a painful, excited squeeze. Eve was lost for words.

'A perfect landing from a first-class pilot!' Eleuia clapped.

The girls stared at each other. Clearly, they were about to meet Santa and they could hardly contain their excitement. But it wasn't a large, jolly man with a white beard who jumped down from the sleigh. Instead, two gloved hands appeared on the wooden rail and a small head peered over the top. An elf gave them a cheery wave.

'You called?' The elf chuckled.

'Genie!' cried Eleuia and Perrie, waving back happily.

The new arrival swung one leg over the sleigh's intricate rail and jumped to the ground with a thud. Unlike Eve and Noelle, she had on her feet a pair of heavy boots with thick laces. Her blue overalls were covered in black smudges of oil and two spanners were jammed into her belt. Genie's face and nose were covered in tiger stripes of grime and, pushed up on her forehead was a pair of dark welding goggles that helped to hold back pink-dipped blonde hair. 'May I present the greatest inventor in Elfland,' Eleuia said with a flourish.

'Ah, please,' said Genie, waving away the compliment.

It was, however, true. Genie combined a command of magic and a mastery of mechanics that had made her well known throughout Elfland for her marvellous inventions. Not least of which was the powerful autopilot she had designed and built for Santa's sleigh.

'At Eleuia's request, and with Santa's permission, I am here to offer you a ride to Elfland Adventures,' she said, turning towards the girls. 'I understand that time is a little tight so climb aboard!'

The sleigh was extremely large, and Eve and Noelle weren't quite sure how they were supposed to just 'climb aboard' without a ladder or a rope. But as they were about to ask, Genie punched a large button and the side of the scarlet sleigh cracked. The doors hinged open just like a private jet and a set of silver steps emerged. Buddy, as ever, was fearless. He bounded straight up the stairs without a second thought and barked back at them. 'Come on! Hurry up!' he seemed to be saying.

Genie went first and the others followed behind. Eve and Noelle held hands tightly. They had a million questions, but they would have to wait. The priority was to get to Miss Jolly before those snoreberries could do any more damage. Lester came last, huffing and puffing reluctantly up the steps that were just a bit too tall for his little legs. As he reached the top, the doors began to close, and he flicked his tail inside just a split second before they clanked shut and disappeared altogether.

With a stuttering and sputtering from the silver exhausts, the great sleigh trembled and rose into the air above the Leaf Factory. There was a loud grinding of gears and it leapt forwards, racing away in the direction of Elfland Adventures.

Chapter 34

An excitable passenger

Just inside the doors, Lester stumbled and almost fell as Genie wrestled the sleigh into gear and it lurched forwards. Frowning, Lester regained his balance and peered around, searching for Genie's troublesome pet.

Lester had been in Santa's sleigh once before and he preferred not to think about *that* particular debacle. So, *he* wasn't surprised by what he saw, and knew what to expect. But Eve and Noelle were already goggling at the luxurious and curious space they found themselves in. There were brass levers, switches and buttons of all shapes and sizes lined up across a wide, gleaming dashboard.

At the controls sat Genie. She was in Santa's seat, and she was the only elf with permission to be there. It was the largest seat in the sleigh, covered in a rich red velvet and draped with warm sheepskin. Eleuia was standing to Genie's right, holding on to one arm of the chair to steady himself as he chatted to her. Perrie perched on her left shoulder, joining the conversation as the sleigh stuttered and backfired.

Genie plucked one of the oily spanners from her belt and spoke into it just like an aeroplane pilot.

'Good evening, passengers, and thank you for flying Santa's SleighWays. Our flight time to Elfland Adventures this evening will be approximately… five minutes. Please hold onto your hats at *all* times.'

With that, she slammed the biggest brass lever forward a notch and the sleigh accelerated smoothly away from the Leaf Factory, skimming the treetops. To the rear of the sleigh, utterly speechless at this moment, Eve, and Noelle (with Buddy in between) sat on a comfortable bench seat which was, like the driver's seat, covered in rich red velvet and stitched with golden thread. Warm fluffy blankets covered their knees, and they craned their necks to see how Genie was operating the controls and to gawp at the trees that rushed past at ever-growing speed. The sleigh was larger and more ornate than they could possibly have imagined, and they marvelled at the precious metals and gemstones that glinted and glittered from every surface.

Genie reached for an engraved silver wheel and,

with some considerable effort, rotated it a little. The sleigh ascended effortlessly to clear an area of woodland where the oldest and tallest trees were to be found. Finally, the elf engineer flipped a large red switch to engage the autopilot and sat back.

Lester, meanwhile, was still nervously peering around the sleigh. Genie never went anywhere without her loyal pet. He had to be here somewhere. Beyond the bench seat where Eve, Noelle and Buddy were enjoying the ride, there was a large area for all the gifts and presents that the sleigh had to carry on Christmas Eve. Lester tiptoed that way and cautiously peered into the corners of the space that was littered with torn and tatty pieces of gift wrap and discarded ribbons and bows. In the far corner, something or someone was rummaging in a pile of screwed-up paper.

Lester froze. Too late. Out leapt Beanie. *This* was Genie's pet. Lester groaned.

As his name suggested, Beanie was, well, bean-shaped, and golden like a shiny coin. He had wild, googly eyes and an ever-grinning, toothless mouth. His arms and legs were thin, but his hands were oversized and shaped like small shovels. Above all, Beanie was lightning fast. In a flash, he had closed the gap to where Lester was standing and excitedly bowled him over backwards into the sleigh's cockpit area.

Genie looked over her shoulder and rolled her eyes. Beanie was always excited to see Lester. Her pet leapt up and, in a blink, had rocketed to the bench seat to welcome the other visitors. The girls and Buddy were fascinated by the ball of energy that skipped and jumped from lap to lap and scurried across the back of the seat behind their heads. Buddy gave Beanie a curious sniff, playfully nudging the bell on the top of his hat. Small as he was, Beanie seemed completely unbothered by the large dog.

Lester picked himself up and dusted himself down. This always happened when Beanie was around. Perrie flitted back to where the girls were trying to keep up with Beanie's movements.

'You are the first people from the human world ever to ride in Santa's sleigh,' she advised them. 'And now, I can let you into a few secrets. The presents prepared in Santa's workshop are shrunk with Diminishing Dust and carefully packed into the sleigh in the right order, just behind where you are sitting.' She gestured to the loading bay and the girls twisted to look at the space where Beanie had been rummaging. Perrie continued, 'Then, the carefully made and wrapped parcels are delivered through chimneys, letter boxes and keyholes all over the world by Santa, assisted by the miraculously speedy Beanie here.' She waved in the general direction of Beanie, but it wasn't one for sitting still very long. Once again, Beanie leapt on Lester for a cuddle and a brief snuggle in his cosy fur. Beanie muttered in loud, incomprehensible squeaks.

Lester peeled the annoying creature off and plonked him down on the deck. 'For the millionth time, Beanie, I have no clue what you're talking about!' Lester declared. Ignoring Lester's obvious desire to be left alone, the funny creature bounced back up and snuggled into Lester's waistcoat. Defeated by Beanie's perseverance, Lester gave him a gentle pat.

'Beanie is just so happy to see you!' Genie laughed from the driver's seat.

'Yes, well right now, I would be happy to see my feather pillow,' Lester said. At this, Beanie jumped up and vanished. In a flash, he was back with a red velvet cushion grasped in his oversized hands.

'How did he do that?' Noelle gasped, looking at Eve. 'He went to get that cushion, but I hardly saw him move!'

'Thank you, Beanie.' Lester chuckled. It was hard to

stay cross with the little creature for long. Lester popped the cushion behind his head and lay back.

'Beanie travels, quite literally, at lightning speed,' Perrie said. 'How else do you think Santa manages to deliver gifts to millions of children every Christmas?'

'Well, we just thought he did it all on his own,' said Eve, suddenly uncertain about all that she had been told.

'Everyone thinks that' said Perrie kindly, 'but it would be a very difficult and lonely job for Santa to have to deliver all those presents on his own. Even the biggest, strongest, and most magical of people need a little help sometimes. Beanie leaps into action whenever there's no chimney for Santa to wriggle down and Santa enjoys Beanie's company on the long journey.

At the controls, Genie reached for one of the brass dials and turned it gently to the left. The sleigh juddered and shivered as it slowed down from its great speed. As it did so, the noise of the rushing wind dropped and suddenly they could hear the faint sound of laughter and music.

'We're here!' cried Noelle.

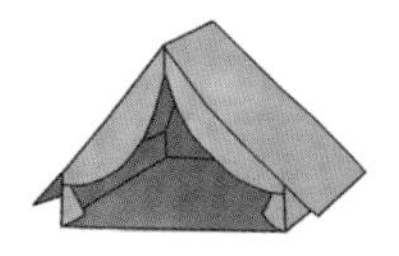

Chapter 35

Touchdown at Elfland Adventures

Both girls rushed to the carved wooden rail of the sleigh and looked over the edge. Genie had steered the sleigh into a gently descending spiral and the passengers were getting a good view of Elfland Adventures below.

There was a brightly burning fire pit in the centre of a large mandala-shaped clearing. The warm currents of air from the fire brought sweet smells of toasted marshmallow to their nostrils and their mouths began to water.

They were looking down on the roofs of tents and other interesting structures. And amongst these, there were many hundreds of tiny people milling about.

Captain Genie once more spoke into her spanner. 'Passengers, we will shortly be landing at Elfland Adventures. Thank you for flying Santa's Sleigh Ways today. Please remember to take all pets with you when you disembark. May I wish you a pleasant onward journey!' Genie stuffed the spanner back in her belt with a flourish and readied the sleigh for landing.

A few flakes of snow began drifting and twirling out of the darkening sky as she searched for a safe spot to land. Delighted, Noelle reached out and caught one of the flakes in her hand. Its beauty was visible for only a brief moment before it melted away in the warmth of her palm.

Satisfied with her choice of landing site, Genie began pulling energetically on the great leavers in front of her and slamming switches into new positions. Eve noticed that Genie stuck her tongue out of one side of her mouth when she was concentrating. She smiled. Noelle did that sometimes too. With Genie at the controls, the sleigh glided gracefully downward and came to rest with a soft thud a safe distance from the bustling crowds of elves. Genie pulled on another lever down by her left hand and the sleigh doors cracked and hinged open. The friendly sounds and sweet smells of Elfland Adventures flooded inside, and her passengers scrambled for the exit.

'Hope you find Miss Jolly before it's too late!' she called after them as they hurried down the silver steps.

The nearest attraction was a very tall and beautifully lit arts and crafts tepee where elf children were busy drawing and colouring with thick colourful crayons at long wooden trestles. *I wonder if they're drawing elves like we did at the Christmas market?* thought Eve and she felt another sudden pang of homesickness. The elves had stopped sketching at the sound of the sleigh's arrival and now gawped at the passengers disembarking. Perrie couldn't tell if they were excited to see Santa's sleigh or Eleuia... or both perhaps? The Wellness Elf was as famous as it got in Elfland, and he received a lot of attention. It was a wonder he hadn't developed a big head.

Eve and Noelle stood and stared. Everywhere they looked there were colourful attractions and happy faces, lit warmly by the great fire in the centre and by thousands of pretty lights. The gently drifting snowflakes caught the light and glittered as they came to rest on elf hats, noses and outstretched tongues.

Above the general hubbub, there was a sudden cry of delight and the new arrivals all spun around to find the source of the sound. An older elf was hurrying in their direction, waving both hands joyfully in the air. She had a welcoming smile and her white, shoulder-length hair bobbed and bounced beneath her elf hat as she made her way nimbly through the crowd towards them. Though Eve and Noelle had not met her, she seemed familiar, and she was clearly very pleased to see them all.

'Miss Jolly!' cried Eleuia, up on his tiptoes and waving back over the heads of the crowd. He was relieved to find the kind and cuddly elf awake and obviously happy. He glanced away and scanned the immediate area for any sign of Cookie or Pretzel. Nearby, he spied a wooden cart, decorated with red bunting. The large sign read 'Sweet Treats'. The cart was overflowing with delicious-looking muffins, candy canes, and platters of the finest fruit in Elfland. There was also a mighty chocolate fountain several times taller than Eve or Noelle. Warm chocolate was cascading over five tiers and it was surrounded with wooden bowls bulging with juicy berries, ready to be dipped.

'Hello everyone!' said Miss Jolly with that warm and welcoming smile. She was a little breathless after hurrying through the crowd and she puffed out her cheeks. 'Oh, dear me.' She laughed. 'I'm not as fit as I used to be!' Miss Jolly took the yoga classes at Elfland Adventures, but she wasn't used to running and dodging through a crowd.

'You are just in time; we are about to open the Sweet Treats stall!' she said, pointing to the line of elves forming in front of the cart. 'It's the most popular eatery here at Elfland Adventures and you can see why! I sometimes think I've enjoyed one too many treats over the years myself.' She chuckled.

'Are those Sweet Treats Café muffins?' asked Eve. The first elf in the queue was reaching for one.

'Why yes, dear, they are!' replied Miss Jolly. 'The most marvellous muffins in all of Elfl—' Miss Jolly didn't have time to finish her sentence.

As one, Eve, Noelle, Lester and Eleuia suddenly pushed past her, almost knocking the kindly elf over in their frantic haste to get to the stall and stop the unsuspecting elf.

'NOOOOOO!'

Chapter 36

Lester leaps to the rescue

Miss Jolly was bamboozled by the sudden panic and bustled after the girls and their Elfland guides. They were already off and running through the milling crowd towards the Sweet Treats stall. They dodged and weaved and bumped and barged, leaving a trail of bemused and disgruntled elves in their wake. Good manners were important in Elfland.

'Whatever is the matter?' Miss Jolly puffed as Perrie anxiously fluttered and buzzed alongside her. There was no time to explain. As the children, Eleuia and Lester charged forward, they could see the elf at the front of the queue lick his lips and begin lifting a muffin to his mouth.

'Stoooooppppppp!' they cried in unison. Everything seemed to be happening in slow motion. The line of elves looked their way but the one with the muffin wasn't to be deterred. His hand kept moving. Several other elves had already plucked cakes from the pile too.

In their desperate haste, Noelle tripped, Eve

stumbled over her, and they both went sprawling on the grass. They looked up from their prone positions and then a quite remarkable thing happened. Lester, in a sudden and surprising show of athletic ability and bravery, bounded across Noelle's back, leapt to Eve's elf hat and sprang into the air. Leaving Eve's little hat bell jingling behind him, he flew like a furry missile, paws outstretched, towards the target.

'Geronimoooooo!' he cried.

The elf at the front of the queue was on the verge of munching the large berry muffin. The sweet smell drifted into his nostrils, and he made ready to chomp into gooey deliciousness. And then, suddenly, his muffin wasn't there anymore.

He bit down on nothing but air and, entirely befuddled, looked down at his suddenly empty hand. Lester hit the ground hard and tumbled, all four of his paws clutching the snoreberry muffin tightly against his furry tummy. He rolled end-over-end several times and came to rest, sitting up, in a dizzy heap surrounded by crumbs. Moments later, Eleuia skidded to a sideways halt in front of the Sweet Treats stall and began apologetically snatching muffins from confused elves.

'Sorry!' he said, offering the baffled elf a glistening candy cane instead. 'Trust me, those muffins taste terrible anyway. Try one of these instead.'

Eve and Noelle, having picked themselves up, joined Eleuia and gathered up the last of the muffins that were held limply in the hands of astonished elves. They returned them to the large basket on the counter and guided confused customers away. Eve held one out to Miss Jolly as she reached the stall.

'Listen!' she said.

'Oh, my goodness!' Miss Jolly exclaimed as the soft snoring of the berries reached her ears. She leaned down and put one ear to the delicious-looking pile of muffins and, sure enough, it sounded like they were all having an afternoon nap. 'This could have been quite disastrous! What if all these elves had eaten these? It looks like you got here just in the nick of time!'

Eleuia lifted the basket from the counter. 'We must dispose of these muffins quickly before everyone at Elfland Adventures is plunged into a deep sleep!'

Lester tottered up, still clutching the muffin he had plucked so spectacularly from the air. 'Don't forget this one!' he said.

'Oh Lester!' cried Eve. 'You were magnificent! Where did that springy leap come from?'

Lester placed the last muffin back in the basket as Eleuia held it out for him. 'Superheroes don't always wear capes you know,' he said, rolling his shoulders like a boxer and sucking in his tummy. 'Sometimes they wear waistcoats!'

Perrie rolled her eyes and Eleuia and the two girls laughed loudly. They were soon distracted, however, by the sound of a familiar voice.

'Coming through! Excuse me! Coming through!' A white chef's hat could be seen bobbing above the crowd and the elves parted to allow an exhausted-looking Cookie to pass. She was breathing hard as she finally arrived at the stall and took in the scene. 'Oh Eleuia, you've been found *and* you're awake!' she said, relieved. 'Thank the gooey, berry goodness!'

Pretzel was puffing along just behind her, lugging a heavy basket which he handed to Ms Jolly. 'Delicious muffins... minus the snoreberries,' he explained breathlessly. He wiped beads of sweat from his brow and swept back a fringe that had become plastered to his head.

So far, the day had been quite a bit more frantic than he'd expected.

Chapter 37

Time to have fun

Cookie and Pretzel busied themselves reassuring the Sweet Treats customers and they were soon doing a roaring trade. Eleuia looked up at the violet sky. It was darkening rapidly, and the Luna Moon would soon rise over the forest. He knew they had only a few short hours to enjoy the attractions of Elfland Adventures.

The inhabitants of Elfland were kind (with one or two exceptions) and they worked hard, year-round, to make sure other people's dreams and wishes come true. It was hugely important work. But Eleuia knew it was equally as important to rest, relax and have fun sometimes. In this regard, Miss Jolly was an expert, and her great joy was to bring happiness and wellbeing to others. He watched as she congratulated Eve and Noelle on their bravery and determination. He saw a little regret in Eve and Noelle's eyes as they glanced around, knowing that they might not have time to play and join in the festive fun here. They were, after all, just children.

Eleuia spoke to them. 'To be selfless and to help others is wonderful,' he said, smiling at them. 'But you must also remember to look after yourselves too. You can't possibly continue to be so fantastically brave and kind and look after others if you don't fill your own cup with happiness and take time to look after yourselves.'

'I couldn't agree more!' cried Lester, wondering where the nearest cheese stall might be. It had been an extremely trying day. He'd been chased by a cat, lost his waistcoat button in a swamp, been shrunk to the size of a dormouse, and had to escape from an evil goblin on the back of an unstable dragon. He certainly felt it was time to look after number one!

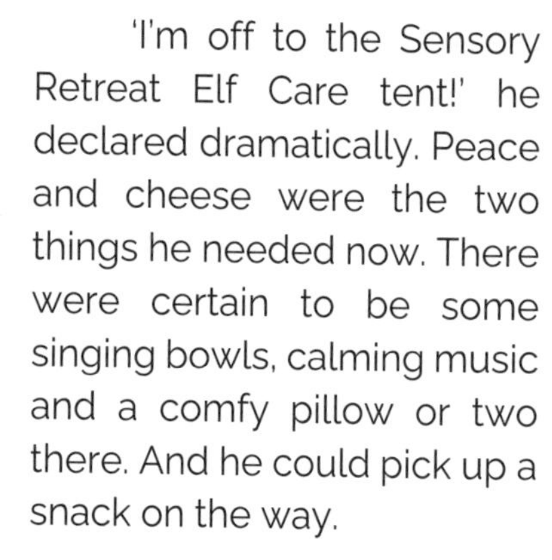

'I'm off to the Sensory Retreat Elf Care tent!' he declared dramatically. Peace and cheese were the two things he needed now. There were certain to be some singing bowls, calming music and a comfy pillow or two there. And he could pick up a snack on the way.

'Well said, Eleuia!' Miss Jolly nodded in agreement, giving Lester a reassuring pat as he passed. 'Miss Eve and Miss Noelle, I think you must have had quite the adventure today! Your Elf Eyes *should* have brought you here immediately, but it seems that events overtook us all. Sometimes, in life, that can happen,' she said thoughtfully. 'Anyway, here you are!' she said cheerily, opening her arms wide and twirling, inviting the girls to look around. 'Elfland Adventures is a rather wonderful place, don't you think?'

There was almost too much to take in. There were musicians, dancers, and acrobats, and so many colourful tents and wooden structures to investigate. It was a little like the Christmas market where they had first spotted Perrie and encountered Mr Arwin, only bigger, brighter and a lot more enticing!

Miss Jolly shot a questioning look at Eleuia, who nodded. 'I do believe we have a short window of time before we visit the Dream Stream and then send you home. Would you like to explore?'

Chapter 38

Eve entertains the crowd

Eve and Perrie wasted no time joining the elves at the main circular stage that seemed lit by thousands of sparkling stars. Here, there was tumbling, balancing and acrobatics. At home, Eve loved gymnastics and, with a renewed spring in her step and encouragement from Perrie, she performed a few somersaults and handsprings across the wooden boards that delighted the elvish audience. Their claps and cheers made her blush and she bowed shyly.

'Bravo!' shouted Perrie, applauding wildly. Buddy barked and leapt in appreciation and began energetically chasing his tail. He received his own round of applause and enjoyed it so much, he did it again.

On a second wooden stage across the central space, there was music. A family of elves were gleefully strumming on banjos and beating tambourines and banging on bongos. A trio of trumpet players, to one side of the stage, had some cool coordinated dance steps and even cooler sunglasses. In front of the stage, the crowd were dancing and tapping along to the beat. The music was so catchy, and the elves seemed very familiar with the tune, for they all joined in with the song. The music, and the beautiful sound of the elves' voices, provided the backing track for the evening's activities and entertainment. The notes swirled and drifted into every corner and merged with the laughter and happy chatter.

As she stood patiently in the queue for the Sweet Treat cart, Noelle couldn't help but tap her feet along to the beat. Cookie and Pretzel were hard at work, handing out muffins, candy canes and plump berries dripping with chocolate. The drama of the snoreberry muffin rescue had been swiftly forgotten. Everyone in the line was so friendly and Noelle fell into conversation with a small group of elves who were on a short break from Santa's workshop. She discovered from them that someone very special was en route to Elfland Adventures that evening, at Mr Arwin's request.

'Santa?' asked Noelle, amazed. 'The real one?' Her new friends nodded excitedly. She scanned the crowd as she shuffled forward in the queue. She *had* to tell Eve!

'Miss Noelle,' greeted Cookie, taking her bowl and piling it high with delicious items from the cart. 'It must almost be home time for you,' she said. At this, her whiskers twitched. 'Where is that cheeky rodent?' she asked, sniffing the air.

'Last seen in the Sensory Retreats tent dabbling in yoga, I think.' Noelle chuckled. 'Today has all been a bit much for him and I believe he's sampling all of the calming, mindful activities he can find.' Noelle thanked Miss Jolly and navigated a way through the crowd towards the stage where Buddy had completely stolen the show and was in his element, showing off *his* best moves to an adoring crowd.

Noelle was almost there when a sudden, loud blast of sound caused her to almost drop her bowl of goodies. The two notes were long, and they echoed through Elfland Adventures, bringing all conversations and movement to a halt. Eleuia stood beside the great fire. He was holding what looked like a long wooden horn with intricate carvings. He brought the thinner end to his mouth, puffed out his cheeks and blew. Again, the two notes sounded loudly and swept across the crowd. All eyes were on Eleuia now and he commanded their attention in the warm, flickering light.

'Elves!' he began. His voice was clear, and it carried to every ear. 'Charge your cups with berry tea and gather here at the firepit. Our distinguished visitor will be arriving at any moment.' A feverish buzz of chatter swept through the crowd.

'Cookie let's gather up all the marshmallows,' suggested Miss Jolly. 'We shall toast them for everyone around the fire.' She could hardly contain her excitement. It wasn't every day that Elfland Adventures received a visit from Santa.

Chapter 39

The elves gather

The elves came into the central space from all directions.

They emerged from the various tents and wooden structures of Elfland Adventures in excited, chattering groups and began to gather around the great firepit where warm, comforting flames leapt and danced. Some perched on the tree stumps that were scattered across the grass, others huddled, smiling, and whispering.

Laughter, music, and dancing had ceased as they awaited the arrival of the guest.

Cookie, Pretzel, and some other keen helpers were making their way through the crowd, offering twigs of marshmallows for toasting and beakers of berry tea. Eleuia stepped from the stage as a very large and ornate wooden chair was carried out and set upon it. He stood with Miss Jolly whilst Perrie fussed and fluttered and straightened the girls' elf hats. She wanted them looking their best. Lester, cheeks already full of marshmallow, was hustling after Pretzel with paws outstretched for a second helping. He knew it would be a bad idea to ask

Cookie, for she still hadn't quite forgiven him. Pretzel gave him a wink, digging to the bottom of the bowl for the biggest marshmallow he could find.

Darkness was descending rapidly now, and the snow had begun to fall in earnest. Fat flakes drifted and swirled around the elves. A wide half-circle of moon crested the treetops and the forest glittered silver in the light.

A sudden cry of delight caused all faces to turn upwards. Across the great crowd, elves were pointing towards the ink-blue sky and the volume of excited chatter rose. Two tiny points of light were blinking rhythmically above them. Red then green. Red then green. They grew larger as they descended, and Eve recognised the sleigh. Its landing lights were on. Genie and her pet had returned with the special guest. Eve reached for Noelle's hand and squeezed it tightly.

The sleigh circled above them, and they could pick out the details of machinery and exhaust pipes. Such was the size of the crowd that there was no safe landing spot to be had and the sleigh banked away and finally dropped slowly behind the canopy of trees a short distance from where they were standing.

They waited and a hush fell over the expectant gathering.

Chapter 40

The remarkable guest

They heard him first. Heavy boots, softly crunching through the snow. Louder. Nearer. And then, he arrived. A huge figure emerging from the shadows and stepping into the warmth of the great fire. He paused for a moment, surveying the scene.

'Santa!'

Miss Jolly stepped forward through the crowd to greet him, her arms thrown wide. The elves shuffled back respectfully to allow her to pass and Santa to enter the vast clearing.

When it came, his voice was deep and rich and comforting. It carried easily through the wintry air.

'Miss Jolly, what a pleasure to see you again. It has been far too long,' Santa boomed, spreading his own arms wide and mirroring her welcome. Their embrace was heartfelt, if a little awkward, for Santa was taller than Miss Jolly and she all but disappeared in the folds of his scarlet velvet cloak. She emerged from their hug and hurriedly dusted down the large wooden chair with a hanky that she plucked from her apron.

Not for the first time that day, Eve and Noelle were dumbstruck. They held tight to each other's hands and gawped as Santa strode past them to take up his seat. Close up, they could see that his familiar red suit was trimmed with white and finished with beautiful golden thread. He seemed to greet everyone with sparkling eyes that shone from behind thin wire-rimmed spectacles. A fabulous white beard – similar to, although shorter than, Mr Arwin's – flowed from his chin and atop his head sat a glorious hat that matched his cloak.

Santa stepped onto the stage and settled himself into the great wooden chair. By the light of the fire, he began to speak to the gathering of elves. They fell utterly silent and hung on his every word.

'Greetings, my friends. It is not often that I make the journey to Elfland Adventures, and I am sorry to interrupt the festivities.' He paused and surveyed the crowd, apparently gathering his thoughts. 'It would seem that, today, my once most-trusted elf, Coletta, descended into such dark jealousy and resentment that she almost succeeded in her attempts to destroy children's wishes and all that Elfland holds dear.'

There was a murmuring of shock amongst the crowd. Santa raised his hand to settle them and continued.

'It is now clear that Coletta will stop at nothing to disrupt and destroy the love and kindness of this land. But for the actions of these brave children and their Elfland guides, she might have succeeded!' Santa gestured towards Eve and Noelle, and they thought they might explode with excitement and pride. There was an eruption of applause and the elves nearest to Eve and Noelle grabbed their hands and shook them vigorously.

Santa raised his gloved hands once more to settle the crowd.

'Coletta has been given many opportunities over the years to learn the error of her ways, but I fear our attempts have been in vain. I have sought the counsel of my trusted advisers and we have decided she *must* return to Astaria to re-enrol at elf school and learn once more what it means to be an elf.'

All the elves began talking at once and there was a further smattering of applause. This had never happened before. No one had ever been returned to Astaria. Above all, the elves realised they would once more be able to enter the Enchanted Forest without fear and this was an enormous relief. Pretzel was over the moon. His trips to collect muffin and cookie ingredients would no longer be such a terrifying experience and he could take his time to make sure he didn't pick snoreberries by mistake.

'As you can imagine, we do not take this decision lightly,' continued Santa. 'Only the hardest-working and kindest of elves are chosen to live and work in Elfland. This is the first time we have seen fit to return any elf to Astaria.'

For a moment, Santa's face fell, and he looked sad. It was a difficult lesson for them all, and even he felt that he had failed. He hoped the Enchantress of Astaria would fare better with Coletta than he had. He was not proud. It was a last resort. But, after hearing that Eleuia had been shrunk by Coletta and the list of Star Wishes lost, no more chances could be taken. Sometimes, perhaps, it was too difficult to help someone when they just did not want to change.

'Has she already gone?' cried one elf boldly from the edge of the crowd.

'Mr Arwin, with powerful fairy magic and the assistance of Tinsel and Bing, has been able to open the portal and escort Coletta safely to Astaria,' Santa reassured them.

The elves rejoiced. Elfland was free of Coletta's nasty influence, and she would hopefully return as the happy and kind-hearted elf she had once been. This was wonderful news for them all and a great cheer arose. Across the great gathering of elves, there were hugs and handshakes, and dancing began as the band struck up again.

Santa looked up at the rapidly ascending moon and then turned his smiling gaze upon the girls. 'Well, well. I do believe it's almost time.'

He pulled a golden pocket watch from beneath his cloak, looked at it, shook it a few times and peered at it again through the wire-rimmed spectacles on the end of his nose.

It was indeed almost time. Within just a few hours, the wishes must be starting their final journey down the Dream Stream.

'Dear Eve and Noelle, shall we take one last trip on my sleigh?' he asked, winking at Eleuia.

The girls found their voices. 'Yes please!' they exclaimed, thrilled at the prospect of another ride in the sleigh, this time with Santa himself.

'Then we must be off,' he announced, climbing to his feet, and adjusting his hat. 'Follow me.' He strode back the way he had come over footprints softened by the falling snow. Eve, Noelle and Eleuia had to quicken their step to keep up as Buddy trotted at their heels and Perrie fizzed excitedly around them.

'Are you coming, young Lester?' Santa called over his shoulder.

Unable to talk through a mouthful of marshmallow, Lester jumped down from his tree stump perch and set off in pursuit, reluctantly leaving the warmth of the fire.

Chapter 41

The Rory Star shines down

The flight had been short but to take that journey with Santa himself at the controls was quite the most wonderful experience. Genie had monitored dials and readouts as Santa navigated the sleigh towards the Dream Stream. With the boss on board, even Beanie seemed a little calmer and better behaved. Lester was grateful for that.

Santa manoeuvred the levers and dials with ease and brought them to a smooth landing.

As Eleuia, Eve, Noelle and Perrie waved their goodbyes, the great sleigh lifted off and turned away. It finally disappeared from view in the light cast by a moon that was now so big it almost seemed to fill the sky.

Eve, Noelle, and Buddy found themselves standing on the banks of a wide stream that flowed through the very heart of the Wellness Woods. It swept over smooth pebbles and spiralled around large rocks that had come to rest on its shores. In the moonlight, the waters were liquid silver, and they gurgled and splashed as they flowed away into the darkness. Just upstream from where the girls stood, there was a graceful stone bridge that carried a cobbled path. It reached over the stream, and it too was shimmering silver by the light of the huge Luna Moon. It had clearly been constructed by skilled stonemasons, for every rock looked to have been carefully cut, smoothed, and placed. Quartz and crystals within the stones set the parapet of the bridge glittering. And there was Eleuia, already on top of the bridge and in position to complete his task.

On the other side of the stream, there was sudden movement in the shadows and Buddy barked a greeting. It was Gizmo. A great tree stretched out over the waters and here was the dragon coiled comfortably in its arms, his wings folded and his head resting easily on his forelegs. The girls were delighted to see him, and they waved a greeting to their new friend. Gizmo's scales glowed warmly in reply and lit up the foliage around him.

Perrie settled on Eve's shoulder and Lester took a few attempts to haul himself onto a nearby toadstool for a better view of events. Magic crackled in the air around them as they all stood silently in anticipation.

Some moments passed and then the musical gurgling of the rushing stream was broken by a new sound. The sound of several pairs of marching feet. Out of the trees, along the cobbled path, came Bow walking confidently with his shoulders back and his head held high. It was a very curious sight for he appeared to be leading two golden letter boxes that were moving under their own steam on skinny legs. They were similar to the one Eve and Noelle had encountered at the entrance to Elfland, but these were far larger *and* grander.

Bow could not have looked prouder of himself. It was a great honour to be selected to take part in this ceremony and to be chosen to oversee the transport of the wishes from the Leaf Factory to the Dream Stream. He spotted the girls, pushed his glasses to the bridge of his nose and smartened his marching step.

The funny little trio stepped up onto the bridge and came crisply to attention just in front of Eleuia. Bow and Eleuia exchanged a few words. With an extravagant salute, Bow turned and hurried off the bridge and along the bank to join Eve, Noelle, and the others. He was pleased to see them and buzzing with excitement.

On the parapet of the bridge, Eleuia reached inside his tunic and withdrew a vial.

'It's the swamp sample,' said Bow quietly. 'Watch this!'

The Wellness Elf plucked the cork from the small glass vial, held it out over the edge of the bridge and slowly began to tip its contents into the rushing stream below.

As he did so, he closed his eyes and spoke softly but clearly to conjure the magic of the Dream Stream.

The first thick drops of swamp mud fell into the Dream Stream and the waters instantly ignited and fizzed before their very eyes. A new source of light flared brightly in the sky above them and the girls glanced up.

'The Rory Star,' said Perrie reverently. She was always awestruck whenever this star shone. 'It's the most powerful star in the Elfland sky. It conducts all the other stars and directs the Elfland magic.'

'It's beautiful,' murmured Eve.

Along the length of the bubbling and dancing stream, neon droplets of every colour suddenly leapt and sparkled. Up on the bridge, now glowing in the light of the magical waters, Eleuia turned to the two strange golden boxes. They shuffled and bent forward slightly as if bowing to him. Then their lids hinged open and Eleuia reached inside.

He emerged with great armfuls of leaves, and he turned to release them over the parapet. They twirled and fluttered to the waters below. Eleuia delved into the golden boxes again and again, releasing thousands of leaves to the burbling stream from wide-stretched arms. They reached the surface with a multitude of soft splashes and began to flow away in the strong current. The words of the wishes, scribed on them with such care at the Leaf Factory, lifted gracefully and danced just above the surface of the water in a golden swirling mist of hopes and dreams.

'Here comes the best bit!' whispered Perrie. 'Look!'

They all turned to look downstream, to follow the path of the leaves and the dancing wishes.

Just when the girls thought things couldn't get more dazzling, a rainbow suddenly arced majestically over the stream. It seemed to grow from one bank to the other and it was the most vibrant that Eve and Noelle had ever seen. As the leaves bobbed and flowed beneath it, they began to fade. They were travelling through some sort of portal just beyond the rainbow. It swallowed them and they disappeared from view, one after another. As each one did so, a new pinprick of light appeared in the midnight sky. Within minutes, the sky was filled with twinkling stars, joining the largest and brightest of them all: the Rory Star. It glowed and pulsed and, as if at its command, the new stars created by the wishes exploded in a dazzling display.

Noelle gasped. 'Like fireworks!' she cried. They all stared in wonder at the spectacular flashes of colour and sparkling explosions.

At the heart of it all, the magnificent Rory Star glittered and shone.

Chapter 42

Time to say goodbye

The last of the colourful explosions rained glittering red sparkles. They flickered and faded away, returning the sky to velvety blackness. The wishes were safely delivered.

Eve glanced across at her best friend. Noelle's upturned face was lit only by the soft glow of the Luna Moon. She was still peering upward, desperately searching for one last spectacular flare of colour.

It was time for Eve, Noelle, and Buddy to leave.

Eve and Noelle had entered Elfland with all the right qualities – kindness, courage, and open hearts – ready to learn about Elfland *and* themselves. If the incredible adventure had taught them one thing, it was that with good friends, courage, and kindness anything was possible.

Bow, fighting back tears, hugged the girls quickly and trudged away. The golden boxes fell into step behind him, and he led them along the cobbled path, back to the Leaf Factory. Lester hated goodbyes. As much as he tried to hide his emotions, he was going to miss Eve and Noelle very much. *I'll even miss that pesky dog;* he thought as Buddy gave his hat one last slobbering lick. His shoulders slumped, the little rat wandered slowly behind the two girls and Buddy as Eleuia led them all away from the stream. Perrie sensed his sadness for she felt it too. They had all had quite a remarkable adventure together. She fluttered around Lester, tweaking his whiskers to try and make him smile.

From his perch across the water, Gizmo launched into the night sky, leaving the branch bouncing and the leaves rustling behind him. He ascended on his powerful wings and circled the sad little group as they walked a short distance from the banks of the Dream Stream. His scales rippled with every imaginable colour, for he was experiencing a mixture of emotions. Sad as he was to see his new friends leaving, he felt happier and freer than he had ever felt before, and it was all thanks to them. Eve had helped him learn that, though people might think he was big and scary, he did not belong in the shadows, unseen and unheard. He had come to accept that sometimes you don't need to be strong and do everything on your own. You need friends, who love you for who you are.

'Goodbye Gizmo.' Eve smiled, waving up to the dragon. He dipped his great head, barrel-rolled across the shining light of the Rory Star and peeled away into the darkness, his rippling rainbow glow gradually fading into the distance.

The girls and Buddy followed Eleuia to a small clearing where elves would sometimes indulge in something called forest bathing. Here, among the trees, were a few comfortable-looking hammocks swinging gently in the Luna Moonlight.

One hammock was already taken, and its occupant sprang out to greet them.

'Remi!' cried Lester, delighted to see the beautiful elf. The Sleepy Elf had more prominent elf ears than the others, poking out from beneath a warm red hat that matched their soft red trousers. Their green top was loose and warm like that of pyjamas and finished with a red collar.

'What a spectacular display, as always,' Remi said, throwing their arms around the two girls for a long hug. Finally, Remi released them, turned and picked up a small wicker basket. 'We have two tired little elves to get safely home,' said Remi, nodding at Eleuia.

At this, Lester hugged Eve's ankle for the first time. She bent down to lift him from the snowy ground and snuggled her nose into his fur. Noelle joined in on the hug to create a sort of awkward human-Lester sandwich.

Perrie fluttered to rest her head on Noelle's shoulder. 'It's been such a pleasure to meet you both,' she whispered.

'It certainly has,' said Eleuia, hearing Perrie's kind words. 'Eve, Noelle and Buddy, a big thank you from me and all the inhabitants of Elfland!' He suddenly felt sorry for Lester who was whimpering quite miserably. Lester was often complaining but he had a heart of gold really. 'Goodbyes are not forever, Lester. They are certainly not the end. It's OK to be sad. It just means we'll miss each other a little until we meet again.'

Remi spoke softly. 'I have a treat for you! Time to make yourselves comfy.' Remi gestured to two hammocks that were side by side and Eve and Noelle clambered in with some difficulty. Buddy leapt in too, setting Eve's hammock swinging wildly. She chuckled sleepily at her beloved dog.

They lay back and gazed up at the Luna Moon.

Remi began humming a lullaby and reached into a small basket to hand Eve and Noelle a gift.

'Elf Eyes!' whispered Eve.

'Indeed,' said the Sleepy Elf softly. 'A warm hug for tired eyes. Eyes that have witnessed quite a few remarkable things today.' Remi tapped both packs with Eve's wand and, together, the girls chanted the now-familiar words.

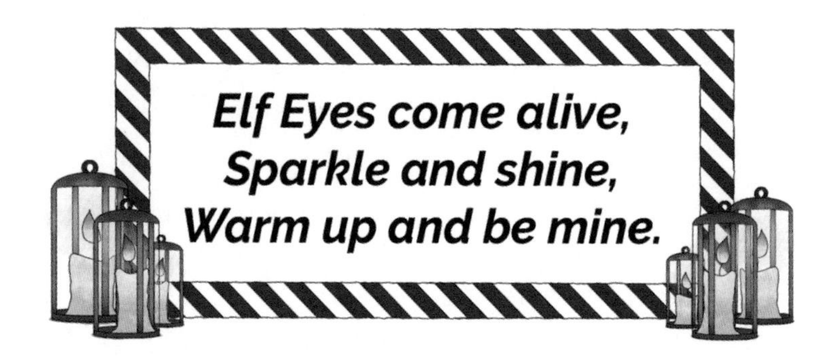

Eve and Noelle placed the masks over their eyes and comforting, calming warmth was activated just as it was before.

They chanted again but this time their words came in drowsy whispers.

Elf Eyes, come alive, sparkle and shine, warm up and be mine.

Remi continued to speak quietly as the girls felt their bodies become heavy in the hammocks. 'Now relax and focus on your breathing. Take a deep breath in and slowly let the breath out. And again, deep breath in and, slowly and gently, let the breath out. Every breath makes you feel more and more relaxed. Repeat this one more time with a deep breath in and slowly and gently, let the breath out. With every breath, feel yourself floating more and more into deep rest...'

Remi's voice was captivating. The girls hung on the Sleepy Elf's every word as they were led by that voice along a rainbow-coloured path and into a magical forest. Their senses were heightened as Remi's words painted beautiful pictures in their minds. 'I am at peace. I am poised, serene and calm. I rest in security and in peace. A great stillness falls over me, and a great calm quiet my whole being. I wrap myself in the mantle of love and fall asleep filled with goodwill for all. Throughout the night, peace remains within me and in the morning, I shall be filled with life and love. I sleep in peace; I wake in joy...'

Eve and Noelle began snoring softly as they drifted into a deep, comfortable sleep.

Chapter 43

Back to school

Siena woke gently from the most wonderful, relaxing sleep she had ever had. Some distant, familiar sound had roused her, but she couldn't quite place it. But then the sound came again, and she realised what it was.

Buddy barked loudly and she suddenly felt his paws bouncing heavily on her legs.

'Buddyyyyy,' she groaned. 'It's too early!'

Beside her, Gabi stirred and poked her head out of her sleeping bag. She was greeted with an enthusiastic Buddy-lick, and she quickly ducked back under the covers.

'I *do* love you, Buddy, but that is not what I need right now!' came Gabi's muffled protest. 'Yuck!'

Sunlight was streaming in through the gaps in the bedroom curtains and they both heard Siena's mother calling up the stairs. It was time to get up and get ready for school.

Reluctantly, Siena and Gabi both emerged from their sleeping bags and peeled off their Elf Eyes. Both girls immediately reached to their heads. There were no elf hats and no neatly plaited hairstyles.

Gabi sprang from her sleeping bag. 'Siena, I had the best dream ever!' she said excitedly, running to peer between the curtains. They were definitely at home.

'The lost wish...' murmured Siena, sharing Gabi's excitement. 'Did you have a dream about a lost wish?' Siena snatched paper and pens from her bedside table and began drawing.

Gabi looked. 'That's Gizmo!' she exclaimed.

'Yes, Gizmo!' screamed Siena excitedly.

'These Elf Eyes are magical,' Gabi said, staring at

the mask in her hands. She couldn't wait to tell Arthur and Albie all about the Elfland dream that she and Siena had shared.

The girls got ready for school at record speed and charged downstairs for breakfast.

'I think maybe I need to try these Elf Eyes for myself.' Siena's mum laughed, listening to the girls describe their dream. She wasn't sure what to make of these tall tales, but she was grateful that the girls were eager for school and ready in double-quick time.

Arthur and Albie were just wandering past the garden gate as Siena and Gabi tumbled from the front door in a jumble of coats, scarves, and bags. As the girls caught them up, they began recounting their dream and their breathless chatter and remarkable story lasted all the way to the school gates.

'So, it wasn't a bumblebee?' asked Albie, finally able to get a word in edgeways. He was convinced he had been right about the fast-moving light at the Christmas market.

'Oh no, Albie. She was so much better than a bumblebee. Perrie was quite magnificent!' Siena declared, recalling the little pixie and her infectious energy. The four children had stopped in the gateway and other children and their parents were having to squeeze past them into the playground.

'Come on, you lot!' called Mr Jones, raising his eyebrows at them. The year five teacher happened to be on gate duty that morning. 'Are you coming in or not?'

'Sorry, Mr Jones!' the four children chorused. They hurried past him, waving cheekily. 'I'll see you in assembly first thing,' he said. 'Miss Clarke has an important announcement for us all. You'd better hurry or you'll be late'

The children looked at each other, shouldered their rucksacks and then turned, scampering across the tarmac towards their classrooms.

Chapter 44

And the winner is...

When Siena and Gabi's class filtered into the school hall, many of the other classes were already there, seated in their designated rows. The girls gave tiny, half-hidden waves to Albie and Arthur. You weren't supposed to wave as you arrived in assembly. In fact, there was a long list of things you weren't supposed to do. These included whispering, groaning, fidgeting, fiddling, giggling, turning round *and* waving. Sometimes, Gabi felt that breathing was frowned upon too.

The term was almost over, and the Christmas tree had been standing proudly at the front of the hall for several weeks now. It was brightly decorated with strands of red and gold tinsel and an entirely random scattering of baubles of all shapes, sizes and colours. It was a school tradition to allow the youngest children free rein with the tree decorations. And it showed, although the overall effect was spectacular. Right at the top of the glittering cone was an angel designed by one of the children in Miss Roberts' class. It had now lost one of its googly eyes and Siena wondered how it could fly in a straight line since one wing was very much larger than the other.

Though cold outside, it was always stiflingly hot in the school hall. The wintry sunshine was streaming in through the windows and dust motes were drifting and dancing in its rays. The children shuffled and muttered and the last one settled. All the teachers had taken up their positions in chairs at the ends of the rows and everyone looked expectantly at the headteacher, Mr Connors. He was a relatively short man, and they could see that today, despite the warmth in the hall, he was wearing his familiar blue three-piece suit. The buttons of his waistcoat were straining a little over his round tummy and one appeared to be missing altogether. Sunlight gleamed on his shiny bald head. Mr Connors was popular with the children and a brilliant storyteller but this morning, it seemed, there were more important matters to attend to and he didn't want to keep everyone waiting.

He cleared his throat, welcomed everyone to the assembly and spoke briefly about the successes of the term. The school choir performed a Christmas carol and they all stood to join in with an enthusiastic, out-of-tune rendition of 'Silent Night'. After that, Mr Connors congratulated children on their efforts and gave out one or two certificates. Finally, he wished them all a fabulous Christmas break, before inviting Miss Clarke to join him at the front.

Miss Clarke was taller than Mr Connors and lit up the proceedings with her brightly patterned Christmas dress and Christmas bauble earrings. She was definitely in the seasonal spirit, thought Siena. Miss Clarke's subject specialism was Art and DT and Siena thought Miss Clarke herself was a walking work of art. She always wore the most interesting outfits, she always looked fabulous, and she was always jolly.

Miss Clarke was struggling under the weight of a large hamper which looked to be bulging with festive goodies. A murmur of excitement rippled round the hall. It looked like it was time to announce the winner of the Design your Spirit Elf competition.

'What wonderfully creative children I see before me,' Miss Clarke began, placing the hamper on the table next to her. 'Throughout this term I have been so excited to see your artistic skills growing and your wonderful imagination on show. The Art and DT projects on display around our school are some of the most marvellous I have seen in all my years of teaching. We definitely have some budding Picassos!' She held her hands out towards them and gave her audience a round of applause. The children and other teachers joined in enthusiastically and after a few moments Miss Clarke held up her hand to settle them again.

'Now,' she continued, 'we have the last award of this term to present today. You might remember that we had a Design your Spirit Elf competition recently. There were so many fantastic entries this year and I was so impressed. It was very difficult to decide on a winner. In fact, I had to ask your teachers to help me.' Miss Clarke paused. The hall held its breath. 'The winner of this year's competition is...' She paused again. 'Siena Brooke!'

Gabi squeezed her friend's hand and grinned excitedly at her. Siena stood up to enthusiastic and loud applause and picked her way out of the row, careful not to trip or tread on any stray fingers. She thought she might burst with pride.

'The design of Eve, your spirit elf, was really detailed and we loved it,' said Miss Clarke, shaking her by the hand. 'Well done, Siena!'

All eyes were on Siena and Miss Clarke. Few if any noticed the flicker of light that playfully darted from the window and came to rest on the hamper. Those that did, assumed it must be the glittering reflection of one of the Christmas tree baubles or maybe the sunlight glinting from a watch face.

But four children in the room *did* notice and they wondered if perhaps it was something more? Arthur sat up straight and met Albie's eye as he whipped around to see if the others had noticed it too. They both stared at Gabi, a few rows away. They all knew what they had seen. At least, they thought they did.

At the front of the hall, Siena was sure. As the applause began to die down, she glanced down into the hamper that Miss Clarke had presented her with, and her heart began to thump loudly in her chest.

There, amongst the selection of festive goodies, was a box. It was dark in colour and covered with white moons and stars. On it, in elaborate writing, were the words... *Luna Eyes*.

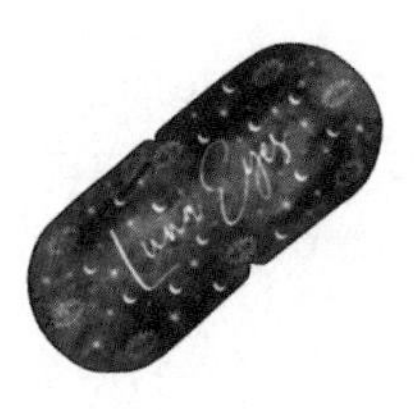

Chapter 45

Dreams *can* come true

After assembly, Siena was told to leave her prize in the school reception area, ready for collection at home time. She carried it dutifully to the low table next to the sofas where school visitors would wait to be invited in. An excited Gabi, Arthur and Albie followed, and the four friends quickly investigated the hamper.

'Elf hats! Two of them,' cried Arthur, pulling them out. The hats were striped in red and green with jingling

brass bells on top. On each hat was embroidered a name.

'Eve and Noelle?' Arthur read.

What else was in this hamper? Siena wondered.

She reached inside, rummaging past the candy canes, festive colouring pad and crayons. 'Look!' She held up a soft toy. It was a dog and it looked just like Buddy!

Gabi laughed. 'Everyone needs a Buddy!'

'Ooh, cake!' shouted Albie, lifting out a little basket of delicious-looking muffins. He did so love cake.

'Hands off!' said Arthur, plucking it from the grasp of his younger brother and placing it back in the hamper next to a box of berry tea. 'This is Siena's prize, remember?'

Siena wasn't listening. She had spied something in the bottom of the hamper, and she delved in to retrieve it. It was long and thin and made of wood and, as she pulled it out from beneath the other items, they could see what it was. A wand, with a carved star at one end.

Miss Clarke poked her head round the door. 'Oh, the excitement shall have to wait!' She chuckled as she began herding the four children away. Unnoticed, Gabi grabbed the box of Luna Eyes and concealed it behind her back. She wasn't leaving that there unguarded.

'Miss Clarke, if you don't mind me asking, who made up the prize hamper?' Eve asked as they made their way along the corridor and back to class.

'If memory serves me correctly, his name was Mr Arwin,' replied Miss Clarke. 'A nice man from the Christmas market. He seemed very enthusiastic about Christmas and was delighted to donate this year's prize.

Now on your way, the bell has rung.'

Miss Clarke strode away, heels click-clacking along the corridor.

'Meet here at break!' ordered Arthur. He and Albie hurried off to their respective classrooms leaving the two girls alone in the hallway. From behind her back, Gabi produced the box of Luna Eyes and handed it to Siena with a grin.

'Heavenly relaxation for your eyes,' she read quietly. 'Transporting you by the warmth of the Luna Moon, to the magical world of Astaria! Tap this pack three times and chant

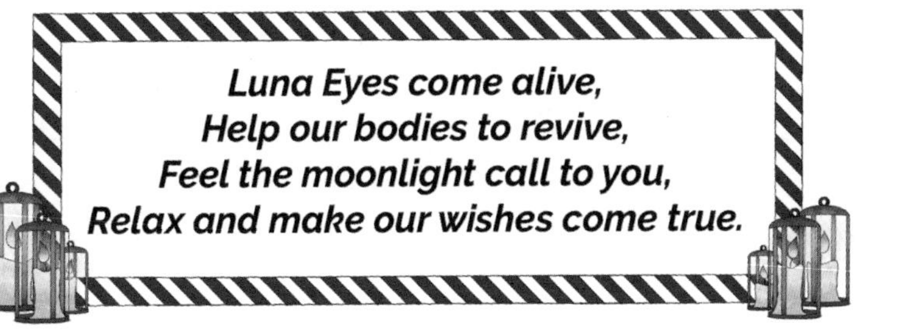

Siena looked at Gabi. 'You know what this means?' she whispered.

'Sleepover time!' squealed Gabi

More than just a book...

The Lost Wish is so much more than a magical adventure book. There are also important messages about resilience, kindness, courage, compassion, empathy, and wellbeing woven throughout.

All the Lost Wish characters have their own personality traits, just like you. Who are your favourite characters and what are they like? Which one reminds you most of yourself today? Who will you strive to be more like tomorrow?

On the following pages, we've made some suggestions for empowering sayings and affirmations to help you start each new day full of positivity and self-belief. You can also find all the story characters along with their personality traits.

Daily Positive Sayings

Today I will ...

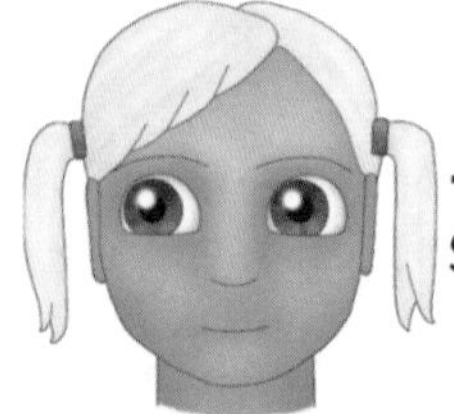

...be kind to everyone at school.

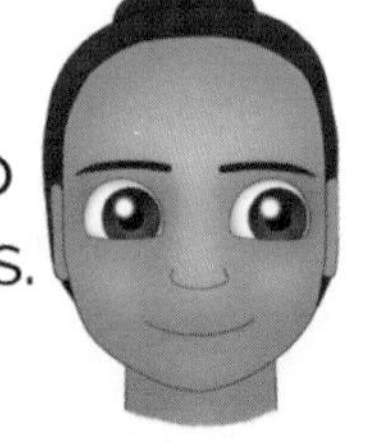

...have the courage to follow my dreams.

...believe in myself and reach for the stars.

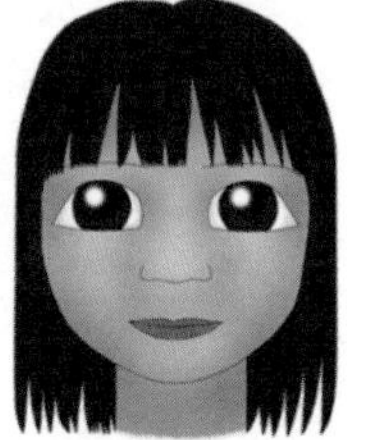

...laugh and help my friends laugh along with me.

...be brave and try something new.

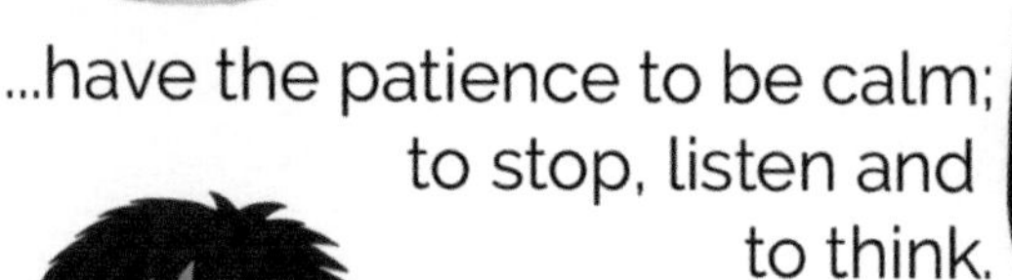

...have the patience to be calm; to stop, listen and to think.

...glow warm and bright like sunshine.

Positive Affirmations

I can be anything I choose to be.

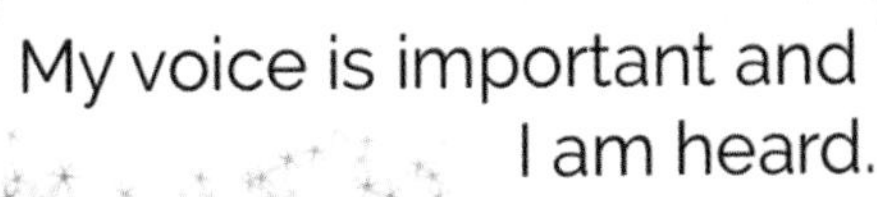

My voice is important and I am heard.

Every new day is a chance to make a fresh start.

I will grow and make new friendships today.

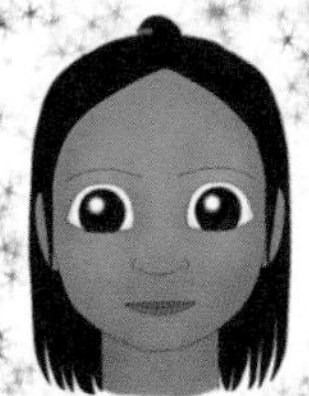

I can always find help when I need it most.

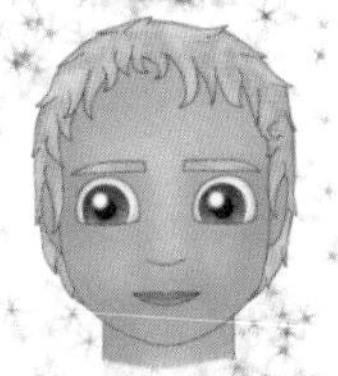

I am loved and respected.

People care about me and I am not alone.

My smile spreads joy everywhere I go.

I work hard and always strive to do my best.

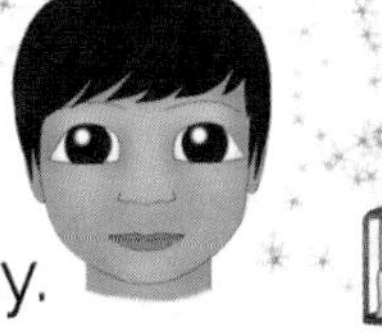

I appreciate every new experience that comes my way.

Positive Character Traits

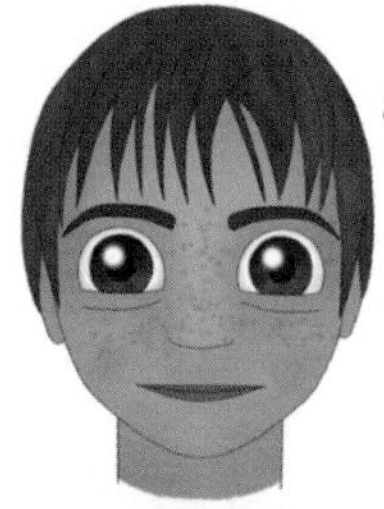

Arthur
Sensible and kind

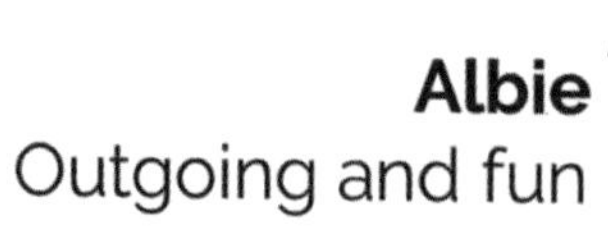

Albie
Outgoing and fun

Siena/Eve
Determined and fearless

Gabi/Noelle
Upbeat and adventurous

Buddy
Energetic and loyal

Miss Clarke
Cheerful and artistic

Lester
Witty and compassionate

Perrie
Supportive and trustworthy

Positive Character Traits

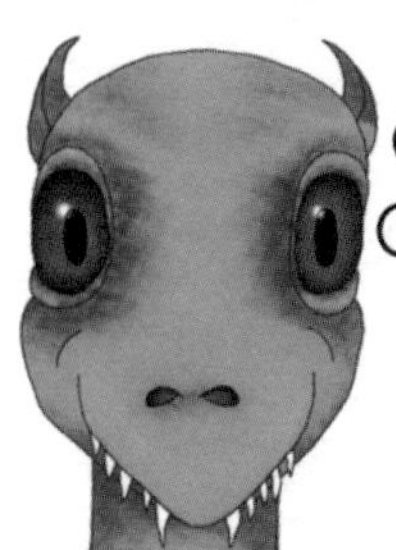

Gizmo
Grateful and brave

Eleuia
Intelligent and focused

Bow
Curious and caring

Mr Connors
Kind and forgiving

Remi
Peaceful and calm

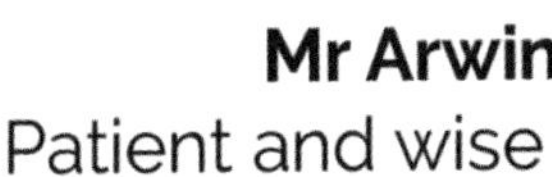

Mr Arwin
Patient and wise

Pretzel
Lively and welcoming

Cookie
Responsible and hard working

Positive Character Traits

Bing
Charming and bright

Tinsel
Empathetic and positive

Beanie
Affectionate and busy

Genie
Confident and inventive

Santa
Generous and gentle

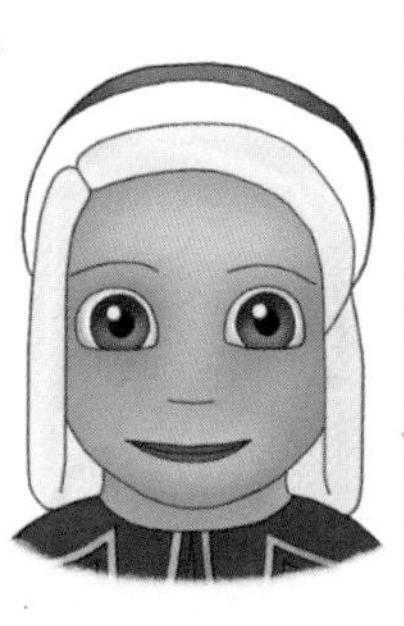

Miss Jolly
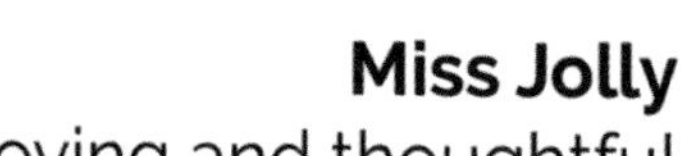
Loving and thoughtful

Coletta
Now bitter and mean but was once joyful and kind

About the Creator of 'The Lost Wish'

The Lost Wish is the vision of Clare Anderson, owner of holistic wellbeing company, Sensory Retreats.

Clare has been in the beauty industry for over 30 years and is a passionate advocate of complete wellbeing for mind, body and soul. In recent years she has been particularly interested in supporting people to achieve consistently restful sleep and deep relaxation.

Evidence has shown that the pandemic lockdown periods had a detrimental impact on the mental and physical health of many adults. But it has also become apparent that children and young people were affected too. Clare realised that, by adapting the Sensory Retreats product range, she could cater for the wellbeing needs of children, to help them relax and to be more present and aware in the moment.

Elf Eyes masks were created to help calm young minds. Their soothing and comforting warmth is a gentle hug that allows busy brains and tired eyes to unwind and relax.

It was an Elf Eyes mask that set Clare on an incredible journey with her daughter, Siena, by her side. Siena had dreamt of a place called Elfland whilst wearing one of the masks and she began to wonder where elves escaped to when they weren't working hard, making presents for children.

Clare developed the concept of Elfland UK. **www.elflanduk.com** is an online portal with a range of products that deliver a host of wellbeing benefits and positive affirmations. Alongside these, are wonderful woodland experiences that focus on the importance of physical activity and sensory stimulation.

Clare's wish is that children everywhere will be encouraged to reconnect with the world around them, using the healing power of mindfulness and nature to relax and recharge.

One further powerful way to do this is by reading. The Lost Wish is a fabulous story, where imagination is limitless, and adventure awaits. Appearing throughout The Lost Wish are engaging characters and exciting events that demonstrate the importance of kindness, courage, and friendship. The book also reinforces the importance of self-belief, something which Clare believes is a powerful and necessary tool to succeed in business, and in life.